Gone In The Pink Of An Eye

A Witch's Cove Mystery
Book 6

Vella Day

Gone In The Pink Of An Eye
Copyright © 2020 by Vella Day
Print Edition
www.velladay.com
velladayauthor@gmail.com

Cover Art by Jaycee DeLorenzo
Edited by Rebecca Cartee and Carol Adcock-Bezzo

Published in the United States of America

Print book ISBN: 978-1-951430-17-7

A dead body on the beach and no suspects. Not the way a sleuth should start her day.

Hi, I'm Glinda Goodall, part time waitress and part time sleuth. Oh yeah, I'm a witch with a talking pink iguana who thinks he's a detective.

A few weeks ago, my seventeen-year old cousin moved in with me (long story). Her passion? Taking photos. She's a witch too, but she refuses to acknowledge it—until she starts to hear voices in her head.

When the dead man turns out to be her photo teacher, I have to help her find out who killed him. This obsession to learn his identity forces Rihanna to embrace her witch side, which leads to seances, ghost sightings, and a whole host of paranormal explorations—and I end up wearing something other than pink. Not a pretty sight.

Please stop by The Pink Iguana Sleuth agency if you need anything. Either Jaxson or I will be there—and Iggy, of course.

Chapter One

"I HAD THE best week of my life," my seventeen-year old cousin, Rihanna, announced, and I couldn't have been happier. Before I explain why, I need to mention how she came to even be here with me. Rihanna's mother had been going through a hard time and needed my family to take care of her daughter. I was hesitant at first to take her under my wing, but I have found these last few weeks with Rihanna to have been wonderful. Like any teenager whose parents didn't provide a lot of supervision, she would take off without notice and not check in. While that worried me sick, she did help solve a murder case! Not bad for a seventeen-year old.

When she showed up on our doorstep, our biggest hurdle had been to figure out where she was going to sleep. My apartment was only a one-bedroom, and my parents' living quarters above the mortuary didn't have a spare room. With a bit of work, Jaxson and I managed to clear a space at the back of our office and convert it into a bedroom. That meant Rihanna kind of became part of our sleuth agency, mostly because the walls were really thin, allowing her to overhear many of our conversations. It was how she was able to insert herself into our last investigation—against our wishes. But as I said, she did help solve the case.

Fast forward a few weeks, and it brings us to now. We were at dinner to celebrate her first week of school.

"What was the best part of your week?" Jaxson asked my cousin.

He always seemed to know when I was spacing out. *Thank you, Jaxson, for picking up the slack.*

"My photojournalism teacher is amazing. I can't believe he went to Iraq to take photos. Talk about dangerous. Not only that, he's traveled all over the US—to New York, Chicago, and Los Angeles. He's been everywhere."

I wonder how Witch's Cove, Florida, a town with a population of two thousand, managed to snag him? "What a resumé. What's his name?" I asked.

For the record, mine is Glinda Goodall. And yes, my mom named me after Glinda the Good Witch, probably because I am a witch—and because she is obsessed with the movie *The Wizard of Oz*. My mom's a witch, too. But enough about us for now.

"Mr. Tillman. The guy is a genius. He gets people. I mean, I swear his shots expose a person's soul."

"That's wonderful. When I went to Witch's Cove High School, there was no class like that," I said.

"Not when I went either," Jaxson added.

Jaxson is six years older than me, and I'm almost twenty-seven. While we attended the same school, I only met him because his younger brother, Drake, is my best friend. Back then, Jaxson was trouble—big time. Now? He's a real sweetie.

"One reason I am so stoked is because I made an A on my photo essay. It's the one I did on Mr. Plimpton."

Ah, yes. Good old Mr. Plimpton, the man from our last

case. He was desperate to sell his ice cream shop, which he eventually did, not that it would do him any good now (long story).

"An A? Wow, that's fantastic. How about your other classes?" I asked.

Before I go on, I have to confess that I love math, and yes, I know I'm in the minority. While I didn't like teaching middle school, I loved the subject.

"You mean math?" she asked with a smile, knowing full well that was where I shone.

"Yes, like math." I cared about history and science and stuff, but math was the end all to be all.

"I made a C+ on my first quiz."

"That's…good."

"For me it is. Trigonometry isn't my thing."

"I can help, you know."

"I know, but I want to figure things out for myself."

"I can respect that."

Jaxson slightly nudged me under the table. I shouldn't have brought up the subject of grades, but I wanted her to succeed. Rihanna was a very independent girl and could achieve anything she set her mind to, but she could sometimes lose focus about what was important in life—like staying safe. However, I didn't blame her for not wanting my help. "Great. Have you made any friends?"

She dipped her head. "Like witch friends or normal people friends?"

"Ouch." Just because her mom never practiced witchcraft, and her warlock dad passed away when Rihanna was only one year old, it didn't mean she hadn't inherited some talent. Just two weeks ago, she'd heard a killer's thoughts. It was real psychic stuff. I certainly don't possess that kind of ability—at least not that I'm aware of.

"Sorry," she said, though from the tilt of her head, she wasn't sorry at all.

"You're welcome to invite anyone over to the office, even after Jaxson and I have gone home for the night. Just don't let anyone look around. We have confidential files here. And make sure everything is picked up by morning in case a client stops by."

She chuckled. "Yes, *Mom*. You don't need to worry about me. I won't mess anything up for you two."

Maybe I was a bit overbearing. "Anything else notable happen the first week of your senior year?" I asked. "Like some cute guy asked to sit next to you at lunch?"

She shrugged. "Hardly. To be honest, I'd rather be outside taking pictures than sitting in class."

"I get it."

She glanced between me and Jaxson. "You mentioned clients. Anyone interesting?"

Our lack of clients was a sensitive topic, and she knew it. Since opening our agency a little while ago, we'd had one paying customer. Thankfully, Jaxson still worked at his brother's wine and cheese emporium located on the first floor of our building to earn some money. While I didn't often pick up a shift at the Tiki Hut Grill, I did so when needed. "No. I meant in case we land a client, I would appreciate it if you made sure the place was presentable by morning."

"Got it."

Just in time, our food arrived, and I dug in. My Aunt

Fern, who owned the Tiki Hut grill, was at the cash register and kept looking our way, though I'm not sure what she expected to see. Fireworks? Between whom?

Before I could decipher her look, the front door to the restaurant whooshed open, and Dr. Elissa Sanchez, our medical examiner, breezed in with a young man who seemed to be around Rihanna's age and looked vaguely familiar.

Rihanna's fork froze in mid-air as she stared at him, acting rather star-struck. For the first time since she'd arrived, she seemed interested in someone her own age.

"Who is he?" Rihanna whispered.

"I don't know, but the woman with him is our medical examiner."

"I would have noticed if he went to my high school, though it is possible, I haven't met everyone yet."

"Give me a sec." Did I mention it's in my DNA to meddle?

Rihanna's eyes widened, and then she grabbed my wrist. "What are you doing?"

"Don't worry." She acted as if I was going to charge over to Dr. Sanchez's table and ask for an introduction. I didn't need to. I had a better source.

When she let go, I pushed back my chair and walked over to my aunt—one of the five gossip queens of Witch's Cove.

"Glinda? What's up?" she asked, knowing full well I was looking for the scoop on something.

"Who's the handsome young man with Dr. Sanchez?" When I recognized that glint in her eyes, I held up my hand. "Don't worry, I'm asking for Rihanna. Sheesh. He's way too young for me."

"Whew. That is a relief. How is that going with your hot man?"

This wasn't about me and Jaxson. "Good, now about the young man in question?"

She grinned. "You can't fool me. I see the way you look at your *partner*," Aunt Fern said.

"Shh." She talked too loud. "Jaxson is my *business* partner, but it might turn into something more. In time. When I'm ready. And assuming no one meddles."

My aunt winked. "I get it. Slow and easy it is. The young man in question is Gavin Sanchez, Elissa's son."

"Mom never mentioned the M.E. had a son."

"He spends a lot of time with his dad, who's a lawyer in Miami. Gavin goes to a boarding school down there, but he just graduated from high school. I believe your mother told me he plans to do a gap year and study with his mom. He wants to become a doctor."

"That's admirable. Rihanna will be happy to hear that. Thank you, dear Aunt."

She laughed. "Go back to your man. By the way, he hasn't taken his eyes off you."

I doubted that. I spun around and returned to the table not wanting to know why Jaxson was indeed watching me.

Rihanna dabbed her mouth with a napkin and held it there. "So?"

Since she was facing the hunky teenager, she probably feared he'd know she was talking about him. "His name is Gavin Sanchez. He's about eighteen and will be taking this next year off to study medical examiner stuff with his mom."

"A year to study dead people? Wow. He must be smart.

And dedicated."

The longing in her voice implied she liked the intelligent type. Good. "I'm not surprised, considering his mom is a doctor and his dad is a lawyer. From what I recall, his folks divorced a long time ago though. His grandparents, Betty and Frank Sanchez own the Candles Bookstore. I bet he'll stop in there now and again." I couldn't help myself but to share everything I knew.

The joy in her eyes was obvious. Ten bucks says it wouldn't take long before those two accidentally ran into each other. I was positive she'd draw Gavin's attention. My cousin was hard to miss. Rihanna was model thin, five feet ten inches tall, and had long, straight black hair. Did I mention she's gorgeous? Okay, I might be a little prejudiced, but she was striking—even with the black lipstick and black eye makeup. I figure the nose stud and eyebrow piercing might attract the younger crowd. It made her mysterious looking, for sure.

Rihanna lowered her napkin. "Thanks," she said with a grin.

Once we finished our celebration dinner, I turned to something else that was weighing on my mind: money. I mentally ran through which shifts I wanted to pick up in order to have some cash available should the need arise. Drake might not be charging us rent, but we had to pay for utilities. Even though Rihanna was chipping in, cooking for an extra person cost money. Aunt Fern said my cousin was welcome to eat at the Tiki Hut for free, but I didn't think that was fair to my aunt.

Working mornings would give me the afternoon off, but the evening shift would allow me to sleep in. Considering no one had died recently and we didn't have any paying clients, I didn't see the need to sit in the office all day doing nothing. To ensure we didn't miss a potential client though, we had a sign on the outside that said to call either Jaxson or myself should we be out and about.

"Time to get you home," I said.

We escorted Rihanna back to our office where she was staying.

"You know I could have walked the hundred feet by myself," Rihanna reminded us.

"I know, but it's nice out, and I'm not ready to call it a night yet." The salted sea air coming off the Gulf of Mexico always soothed my soul.

We reached the steps that led up to the second-floor office. "Then I'll say thank you and goodnight. I have some reading to do. And yes, I'll look over my Trig again to see why I botched the quiz."

On a Friday night? She acted too much like me. "Good for you. If you have time, you could message your mom."

That had been a sore subject. I think Rihanna wanted to pretend as if she hadn't grown up with a single mother who basically chose to avoid life through drugs.

"I will. Someday. When I'm ready."

She really did sound like me. I know my mother had left a few messages for her sister since Rihanna's arrival to let her know how well her daughter was adapting, but getting a message from her only child might help with her recovery.

Once Rihanna was safely inside, I turned to Jaxson. "Thanks for joining us."

"You know I'm always up for a free meal."

I chuckled. It hadn't been free for me. "See you tomorrow then?"

"Yup. Are you going to work at the office or at the restaurant?"

"I think I'll do a little organizing at the office first. Then I might pick up an evening shift."

He clasped my shoulders, leaned over, and kissed my forehead. "Night, pink lady."

My heart dropped to my stomach before slowly bouncing back again. I was sure his gesture was platonic but having his large body close to mine did something to my insides. "Night," I managed to choke out.

Just so you're in the loop, the pink lady nickname referred to the fact that I only wear pink. Rihanna, on the other hand, only wears black.

As Jaxson slid into his car, I headed back to my apartment situated above the restaurant. On my very short walk back, my cell rang, but I didn't recognize the number. "Hello?"

"Is this The Pink Iguana Sleuth Agency?"

"Yes, it is." My hands actually shook. Could this be a client? We'd done nothing to warrant a complaint.

"My name is Isobel Holt. Two days ago, my house was broken into."

I hadn't heard. "I'm so sorry. How can I help?"

"The sheriff is investigating the theft, but he says he has no leads. One of the items stolen was a very sentimental piece of jewelry that belonged to my mother. I'll pay whatever your going rate is to get it back."

I was almost about to say that I was pretty good at finding murderers, but that I had no experience with thieves.

Fortunately, my filter remained in place. "We'd be happy to help. Can you stop by the office tomorrow morning? Say at nine?"

"I'll be there. And thank you."

I practically skipped home. We had our second client! Things were definitely looking up for The Pink Iguana Sleuths.

But hey, success comes in small stages.

"Are you a relative of the necklace?"

He had every right to ask. The one locator spell had been to find Rihanna. Normally, an empath would be needed to connect to the missing person. Since I was related to Rihanna, I gave it a try. I found her car, but not her, which I considered close enough. A necklace was altogether different. It was an inanimate object. "I'm hoping there is a spell for items."

"Maybe there is." I could almost hear the smile in his voice.

"I called to let you know that we are meeting with our client at nine tomorrow morning."

"I'll be there."

I never doubted it. "Night."

We disconnected, and I sighed. It was great to be able to share such concerns with another person without being made fun of—more or less.

Happy, I went into the living room to fill in Iggy.

"DO YOU HAVE a picture of the stolen necklace?" I asked Mrs. Holt the next morning.

"Yes. My husband insists on insuring everything." She handed me a beautiful eight by ten color photo, and I couldn't help but whistle. "This is exquisite."

"You can see why I'm willing to pay to get it back."

"I most certainly can."

"Tell us about the robbery," Jaxson said. He had his tablet poised to take notes.

"When my husband, Richard, stopped home from work early the other day, all of the doors and windows were still locked, but the safe had been emptied."

That was strange. "Who else has a house key?"

"No one but the two of us."

"A housekeeper, a relative, or a next-door neighbor, perhaps?" I asked.

"No."

"Let's assume for a moment that someone was able to make a copy of your key without your notice," Jaxson said. "What else was taken?"

She handed us a list. "A fair amount of cash that we kept in the safe and some other jewelry that I had in there as well."

"No electronics or anything else?"

"No."

The jewelry could be pawned, but it also could be traced, assuming the thief tried to fence it locally. "I assume the sheriff checked the pawn shops for the jewelry?" I asked.

"He said he did."

"Was this necklace kept in the safe, too?" I asked.

"It was."

This sounded like an inside job. I wondered if maybe the husband took the items because he was in some kind of financial trouble. Jaxson would have to do his magic and search for information about Mr. Holt's financial health. "I'm guessing only you and Mr. Holt have the combination?"

"Of course."

Jaxson leaned forward. "Who do you suspect?" he asked.

"No one." Her lips pressed together.

This wasn't looking good, and I could understand her

frustration. "May I ask what you and your husband do for a living?"

"I do a lot of volunteer work, but my husband is a financial advisor."

The stock market had been in a free fall lately. Maybe Mr. Holt didn't want to tell his wife about some big loss, so he'd faked the robbery. "Jaxson and I will look into it."

"Thank you so much, but may I ask where you plan to look if the sheriff is stumped?" she asked.

Good question. I had to come up with something. "I'm sure you know that I am a witch, so there are things I can do to find the necklace." That was a stretch, but I didn't want Mrs. Holt to think we weren't qualified, even though that might be the case.

"That's what I was hoping you'd say." She pulled out a scarf from her purse. "I don't know if this will be of any use, but it belonged to my mother. Maybe you can make a connection to her with it."

That was doubtful, but I wouldn't tell her that. "I'm assuming she's passed on?" I never liked asking if she was dead. That sounded so final.

"She is."

"We'll get right on it." It was possible the scarf would help—just not for me.

"Thank you. Let me give you my number should you have any other questions."

After we took her information, she left, and I spun to face Jaxson. "Did I promise her too much?"

"I couldn't say, but she left happy."

I walked over to my desk, turned the chair around, and

dropped down. "I don't know where to begin. Usually, we have a body. At least with that, I could ask Mom to contact this person from the beyond. And if the medical examiner refused to give up her information, I could always use my pink crystal to figure things out for myself. But with a lost necklace? I'm in foreign territory here."

Jaxson stepped over to me and held out his hands. I wasn't sure what he wanted me to do, but I'm guessing I was to take hold, which I did. He pulled me to my feet and gathered me into an embrace.

"Stop obsessing and just breathe. We'll figure it out. Okay?" He smiled and then stepped back.

Those words of encouragement helped. "Thanks."

"Have you eaten today?" he asked.

"Eaten breakfast?"

He chuckled. "Yes, breakfast. It's barely ten. I figured it was too soon for dinner."

He always liked to joke. "No, I haven't eaten. I was too nervous this morning."

Iggy crawled out from behind the sofa. He'd been hiding, because I had asked him not to show himself when we had a client. Though he could roam about the Tiki Hut, having him do so in an office might be distracting to some clients. "We going to the diner?" he asked, sounding very excited for the adventure.

"Sounds good to me."

Because Rihanna was out on one of her photo-taking safaris this morning, Jax and I walked the short distance south to The Spellbound Diner. I had no idea if the owner, Dolly Andrews, another gossip queen, would be there, but I wasn't really looking to pick her brain. At least not today.

Once we were seated, we ordered, though food wasn't first and foremost on my mind for a change. I did, however, remember to order some lettuce leaves for Iggy, as opposed to the last time when I forgot.

"Tell me your take on this case," Jaxson said.

"As much as I hate to say it, my primary suspect is the husband since I'm not sure a thief can both unlock and then lock a door. It screams an inside job to me."

"Unless, as you implied, someone made a copy of the key."

I snapped my fingers. "Like when you give your keys to a valet."

"Yes, but where in Witch's Cove is there valet service?" he asked.

He always had to find the flaws in my thinking. "Nowhere."

"If the husband did do this, I would think he'd have made it look like a robbery. Maybe toss a few drawers, break a window or two, and steal something not in the safe."

"Another excellent point," I said. "What are you thinking?"

"Witchcraft."

I chuckled. I was usually the one to think along those lines. "Really? Why is that?"

"Both you and Iggy are capable of cloaking yourselves."

"Iggy can do it on command. Me? It takes too much out of me."

"Then a more experienced witch or warlock perhaps."

"How does cloaking help?" I asked. "Sure, this person

could get in and out without being seen, but how did he unlock the doors or relock them afterward? Or know the safe combination for that matter?"

"The safe combination is easy."

Our server carried over our coffees. "Food will be up in a minute."

"Thanks." I was fascinated by Jaxson's theory. "Go on."

"If the thief couldn't be seen, maybe he followed Mr. Holt inside and watched as he opened the safe."

"I like it. I'll ask Mrs. Holt how often either of them accessed the safe. If it was once a week, then the thief would have to stay cloaked for a long time. I'm not even sure if Gertrude Poole in her prime could have done that."

"Thanks for spoiling my brilliant logic," he said.

I laughed. "Just giving it back. I'm wondering if some warlock or witch with enough power could mentally unlock and then lock a door or open a safe for that matter?"

"That's a scary thought."

"I know." Jaxson sipped his black coffee while I dumped in two creams and some sugar into mine. "Since I want to stop at Hex and Bones Apothecary to see if Bertha knows of a locator spell for an object, I'll also ask if she's heard of any witch who has bragged about being able to work with locks."

"I wouldn't tell anyone if I could do that," he said.

"Neither would I. Some unscrupulous person might blackmail me into breaking and entering or rather just entering since no breaking would be necessary."

Dolly rushed over. "I didn't see you two come in," she announced a little out of breath. "Tell me something good. It's been rather dry around here lately."

I chuckled. Dolly lived for gossip. "We have a client!"

"Slide over." She motioned to Jaxson. "Give me the five W's."

"I can't say who. That is confidential, but I'll tell you this woman's house was broken into—or rather wasn't." I waved a hand. "It's complicated. But someone opened the safe and grabbed some cash and jewelry. More specifically, a gorgeous necklace with diamonds, rubies, and amethysts that had belonged to her mother was stolen."

Dolly whistled. "How terrible." She wagged a finger. "When did this happen?"

That was one of the five W's I'd forgotten to mention. "A few days ago. And yes, Steve is on it. I'm surprised Pearl didn't tell you."

"Pearl is out of town for a few days. Boy, do I miss her." She shook her head. "You know…come to think of it, I had a customer in here a few days ago from Palm Ridge. She and her husband had their safe broken into the week before."

Palm Ridge was one town to our south. "Did she say how the thief got in? Like did they smash a window or break down the door?"

"That's the weird part. The doors were locked when they arrived home."

Whoa. "Did this happen during the day?"

"Yes. I know that look. What gives?"

I didn't want to give too many details, but I had to disclose something. "Our client's home also had the doors and windows locked. I have no idea how the person got in and out."

"We thought it might be an inside job," Jaxson said, "but

two such similar cases makes that unlikely."

"I agree," Dolly said.

My cell rang, the ring tone indicating it was my aunt. She rarely called during the day. "I should take this." I held up a finger to Dolly. "Hey, Aunt Fern."

"Oh, Glinda. You have to come over to my place right away. It's Rihanna."

Sobbing sounded in the background. "Oh, no. What happened?"

"Someone died on our beach, and Rihanna recognized him."

My gut churned. "We'll be right there."

Chapter Three

"**W**HAT HAPPENED?" DOLLY asked, her face full of concern.

"Apparently, someone was found dead on the beach. Rihanna saw the body and recognized him."

"Who was it?"

"I don't know." I glanced up and spotted our server carrying over our order. "Can we get our food to go?"

"Of course."

Dolly slipped out of the booth and quickly packed up our meals. "It's on the house today. Go take care of Rihanna."

"Thank you." I would definitely return and pay her.

Jaxson grabbed our To-Go bags, and we rushed down the street toward the Tiki Hut Grill.

"Can I have my lettuce at least?" Iggy complained.

"As soon as we get to Aunt Fern's I'll give you some." Sheesh.

Jaxson and I half jogged, half walked. When we entered the restaurant through the back, we practically ran up the stairs to Aunt Fern's apartment. I knocked and then went in.

Rihanna looked up, and my heart cracked. Seeing a dead body for the first time would be traumatic. I sat down next to her.

Out of the corner of my eye, I watched Jaxson dig out the lettuce leaves for Iggy. It was no wonder my familiar adored him. Jaxson then sat down on the chair opposite the sofa but said nothing.

I took her hand and squeezed. "Tell me what happened."

"I…ah was taking pictures of some seagulls when I heard the sirens."

I looked up at Aunt Fern. She hadn't mentioned that. Then again, she was probably pretty shaken up at seeing Rihanna so distraught.

"Then what?"

"The sheriff came, and then a ton of people huddled around the body."

"How far away were you?" I asked.

"Just down the beach. I didn't know what was going on at first. As I got closer, I took shots of the crowd, but when I finally made it over there, I spotted a man, face down, on the sand."

"That's horrible. Could you tell how he died?"

She shook her head. "I didn't see any blood or anything, but the medical examiner was there with Gavin, and they mostly blocked my view."

I hissed in a breath. I hope the young man was ready for that. "When Steve saw you, did he tell you not to take pictures?"

"Yes. He said it was a crime scene." She rolled her eyes. "Whatever. It was this deputy guy who was keeping people back, but when the medical examiner asked that they turn the body over, I nearly lost it."

My heart crashed into my stomach. "Who was he?"

"Mr. Tillman, my photojournalism teacher."

"Oh, no. I am so sorry." I ached for her.

Tears streamed down her face, causing her mascara and eye makeup to run. Now I understood why she was so upset. Mr. Tillman was her favorite teacher.

"You have to find out who did this," she choked out.

"He might have died from natural causes."

"No. He was too young."

Sadly, young people died all the time. "How old was Mr. Tillman?"

"In his early forties."

Such a shame. "If he was murdered, the sheriff will find out who did this."

"Maybe, but you have to help. You can learn things that he can't. And I'll help."

"Rihanna," Jaxson said. "You did an amazing job the last time, but assuming this wasn't an accident, this person, or people, might really be dangerous."

"I don't care."

While I could give her rules about when she could leave the house and when she had to stay home, short of me sleeping on an air mattress by the office front door, I couldn't control her, and that scared me to death.

"Jax and I will try to help, okay?"

She nodded reluctantly. Oh, boy. I had the sinking feeling there was no way I could stop her from investigating on her own though. After all, she did aspire to be a photojournalist.

For the next hour, we chatted with her even after Aunt Fern returned to her restaurant. I think she was uncomfortable with all that grief. The strange part was that Rihanna had only known Mr. Tillman for a week. All I could say was that he must have been one inspiring teacher.

I looked over at Jaxson, uncertain what we could do. We had a client, and I needed to find out if there was a locator spell for the missing necklace. If we could wrap up that case, we could turn our attention to Mr. Tillman's demise and maybe help Rihanna cope with her grief. I mouthed the word, *help*.

"Rihanna," Jaxson said. "How about we go back to the office?"

She wiped a palm under her eyes. "Okay."

Since I had ordered too much food, I would share my meal with my cousin if she was hungry. With our To-Go bags in hand, and Iggy snug in my purse, we headed back.

"I'm going to lie down," Rihanna said once we arrived.

"That's a good idea."

After she disappeared into her bedroom, we heated up our breakfast, but I wasn't really in the mood to eat much of it.

"We need a plan," Jaxson said.

"I know, but I don't think there is much we can do until we learn what caused this man's death."

"That will take the medical examiner a good day or two, I suspect," Jaxson said.

"Yes. In the meantime, I want to stop over at the Hex and Bones for that spell."

"You go, and I'll watch Rihanna," Jaxson said.

"Thank you." Only then did what Dolly had told us sink in. "Do you think Steve knows about that robbery in Palm Ridge? The two crimes seem similar."

"He might. How about when you get back, we'll figure

out how to handle it? I doubt our esteemed sheriff's department needs us bothering them over a theft when they have a death on their hands."

"You're right. I won't be long." I turned to Iggy. "Do you want to come to Hex and Bones with me?"

He looked over at Jaxson. "I think I'm needed here more."

That was such a mature attitude. "I'm sure Rihanna will appreciate it."

I walked over to the occult store. Usually, I was excited to expand my witch-based knowledge, but right now I was worried about Rihanna. I hoped for her sake that her teacher's death was from natural causes. Even if Dr. Sanchez was working on the body right now, I had no idea when I'd learn of her findings.

Inside the store, several customers were milling about. When I spotted Bertha, the owner, behind the counter, I rushed over to her.

"Glinda. What's wrong?"

She always could read me quite well. "Remember the locator spell you gave me to help me find my cousin?"

"Yes. It worked, right?"

Not exactly, but her abandoned car convinced me that my cousin was in trouble. "She's home safe now, thanks to you. This morning, someone died—or was maybe murdered—and his body found on the beach. Rihanna not only saw him, but she knew the man."

"Oh. My. Dear. How is she holding up?"

"She's pretty badly shaken," I said.

"How can I help?"

"I need to finish our current case before I can be with her."

"What's this case?" she asked.

"Our client's house was broken into, and a sentimental necklace was stolen. I was hoping there is a spell to maybe find it."

She sucked in a breath. "I'm sorry, but there isn't, at least not that I know of."

I was afraid of that. I pulled out a scarf. "This scarf belonged to the necklace's owner. Do you know of anyone who might be able to touch it and see—if that's the right word—where the jewelry piece might be now?"

"I would ask Gertrude. Touching objects and getting a sense of a person would require a brilliant psychic mind."

And Gertrude was the best psychic in Witch's Cove. "I should have thought of her. One last thing. Have you ever come across anyone who can open and close locks with his or her mind?"

"No! If there was such a person, I imagine he would belong to a dark cult, and I want nothing to do with their kind."

"Me neither." I stuffed the scarf back into my purse. "Thanks for suggesting Gertrude."

"Good luck."

I headed across the street to the Psychics Corner. I had no idea if Gertrude would be free to help, but I had to give it a try. When I entered the main area, Sarah was at the receptionist's desk.

She looked up and smiled. "Glinda. Looking for Gertrude?"

Was I that predictable? Probably. "Is she in?"

"I'll check." She tapped away on her computer. "You're in luck. She has the next half hour free."

"Thanks." This time I would insist on paying. No more free consultations.

At Gertrude's door, I knocked.

"Come in."

I entered. "Hey, Gertrude. I'm here for a consultation." That meant I was a paying customer.

"Glinda. Nice to see you. Have a seat. Can I get you some tea or water?"

"I'm good."

I had several things I wanted to discuss with her, so I launched into what I needed. I explained about the stolen necklace and the scarf. "Are you able to hold an item that belonged to the necklace's owner and see any images?"

"I might be able to help you with that."

I honestly hadn't expected her to say that. I handed her the scarf. She held the gauzy material in her hands and closed her eyes. Gertrude started to rock back and forth, which I took as a good sign. She eventually opened her eyes. "The woman must have passed a long time ago. The scarf has been handled often since then."

My body sagged. "So nothing?"

"I can't be sure. I'm seeing water."

"We live on the Gulf of Mexico. Can you narrow it down a bit?" I asked.

She shut her eyes again. "It's a river. Does that mean anything to you?"

Considering most coastal Florida towns had rivers running through them, it didn't help much. "Not really, but I appreciate the effort."

"I'm sorry."

"That's okay. There's something else though. I can't be sure, but it appears as if the thieves have struck more than once. Both times, the windows and doors to the house have remained locked."

"I would assume they had a key."

"That was my first thought, but could it be done with witchcraft? I was talking with Bertha, and she thought it might be some kind of black magic cult that has the ability to open doors using their minds."

Gertrude's stare nearly cut me in two. "I might have an idea, but I don't want to say anything until I've checked it out."

That was all I could ask. "Thank you." I stood, and she handed me back the scarf. "I'll pay on the way out," I said.

"Thank you and good luck."

For the first time in a long time, she didn't say not to bother with the payment. Since she had answered all of my questions, I left. After I settled up what I owed, I wasn't quite ready to return to the office. Needing something sweet to settle my racing mind, I went to The Moon Bay Tea shop. I thought Rihanna, and maybe Jaxson, would appreciate one of their pastries.

Inside, I stepped up to the counter. A young girl was there, but I didn't see Maude, the owner. I ordered two sweet iced teas, one for me and one for Rihanna. For Jaxson, I asked for an unsweet tea. I then picked out three different pastries, though if he didn't want one, I'd be happy to help him out.

Just as the girl handed me my order to go, Maude emerged from the back room.

"Glinda." She glanced down at the bag. "I take it this is comfort food? I heard about Rihanna knowing that poor man on the beach."

News sure traveled fast. "Mr. Tillman. Yes. He was her photojournalism teacher at the high school."

"That is terrible. Who would want to murder him?"

Was she guessing he'd been murdered, or did she know something? "Did Pearl tell you he was killed?"

Yes, I know Dolly mentioned that Pearl was out of town, but perhaps she'd returned or had spoken with Steve first and then called her close friend.

"Not Pearl. She's out of town. I don't reveal my sources, but I heard the poor man was tasered—in the back, no less."

I thought stun guns only, well, stunned a person. "That's what killed him?"

"The autopsy isn't back, but Steve thinks the shock might have prompted a heart attack."

That would explain the lack of blood. "Good to know. Thanks." I was really curious about the identity of this anonymous source, but most likely, I'd never learn a name.

For the first time in a long while, I wasn't in the mood to chat about possible suspects. I grabbed my drinks and sack of pastries and headed back to Rihanna. I might have to think about hiring a therapist for her. If I had seen one of my high school teachers dead, I would need one.

Chapter Four

WHEN I STEPPED into the office, Jaxson was on his computer. Since I didn't see Rihanna, I had to assume she was still in her room.

He looked up. "Comfort food, I see."

He knew me well. "Yes. Sweet teas for me and Rihanna and an unsweet one for you. I bought three pastries, but if you don't want one..."

"Not on your life."

I smiled. I set the food on the coffee table and then removed the scarf from my purse. I didn't want anything to get on it. This item seemed almost as valuable to Mrs. Holt as the necklace.

"I have news about Mr. Tillman," I said. "I'd like Rihanna to hear this."

I was about to get her, when Jaxson waved me off. "I'll get her."

My cousin stepped out of her room a minute later and looked even worse than when I left. I wish there was something I could say that would help.

"Jaxson said you have news about Mr. Tillman?"

I patted the sofa seat next to me. "Yes, and I brought you an iced tea and a pastry, in case you didn't eat any of the breakfast."

"Thanks." I was surprised when she grabbed one of the rolls.

"Mind you, I learned this via the gossip chain, but I believe your teacher was murdered."

She sucked in a breath. "By whom?"

"I wish I knew, but someone tasered him in the back."

"Tasered?" Jaxson said. "I didn't know that could kill a person."

"Maybe he was wet, and the tasering caused him to be electrocuted," I said, not sure where that thought came from.

"Let me check that out." He went back to his computer and started typing.

"We'll find out more after the autopsy," I said.

"Any clues?" she asked.

"No. Again, Dr. Sanchez has to do her magic first. Then we can start asking around. Did Mr. Tillman mention if he had any family nearby?"

"No."

"Did you see him hang out with any teachers? Maybe one of them has an idea why Mr. Tillman was attacked." For all I knew, he might have been into something nefarious or else people from his past might have come after him. Certain photos could be used as blackmail, not that I was about to accuse this poor soul of any such thing.

Rihanna pressed her lips together. "I only saw him during class."

Too bad. "Do you have a picture of him by any chance?"

"I do. On Friday, we did portraits, and Mr. Tillman posed. We did side lighting, overhead, and Renaissance lighting. I'll grab my camera." With more energy than I'd seen from her since Mr. Tillman's death, she disappeared into her room and then returned, her head down as she scrolled through the photos. "This shows his face the best, but I don't know what good it will do."

"I'm not sure either." I looked at his image. He was an incredibly good-looking man. Medium brown hair, light bluish-gray eyes, and a devastatingly good smile. "What a shame."

"I know." Rihanna took the camera back.

"The article claims that over a thousand people have died from being tasered," Jaxson reported.

"Does it say how old the people were? Perhaps only those with weak hearts are susceptible."

"No. I'd be guessing, but if the police were involved, I would think the targets were probably young, not that old people can't be criminals."

"You're probably right." From Mr. Tillman's broad shoulders, he looked like a man who worked out, so I wonder how he was caught by surprise? Hopefully, the autopsy would show if there had been a struggle.

In relative silence, I drank my tea and enjoyed my Danish. As good as it was, when it was finished, I was still empty and unfulfilled. Not only did I not learn about the person who had killed Rihanna's teacher, but I was pretty much at a dead end in regard to Mrs. Holt's situation, too. I still had hope that some psychic out there could connect with that scarf.

"Rihanna, can you toss me that scarf." It was next to her, and I didn't need her spilling anything on it.

"Sure." She picked it up and froze. A few seconds later,

she dropped it.

"What is it?"

"Nothing." She balled it up and tossed it to me. I wasn't psychic, but I could read people. "Did you just see something?"

She didn't answer, and that was telling in and of itself.

Jaxson moved next to her. "You can tell us, honey. It's okay."

"It was nothing. I think it smelled like something familiar."

"Like what?" I urged. I hadn't seen her lift the scarf to her face and inhale.

"I can't really describe it." Rihanna huffed out a sigh. "Fine, I did see something."

"What?"

"It was an image of the back of a man's head, one with a lot of blond curls."

I glanced over at Jaxson and then back at Rihanna. "Have you ever touched anything before and seen something."

She looked down at her hands. "Maybe."

Rihanna wasn't raised to think in terms of witchcraft, but I'd bet anything that she had a lot of untapped talent. "If you ever see things again, let us know, okay? It could be important."

"I will. Can I go now?"

I didn't want to make her any more uncomfortable. "Sure."

When she entered her room, I turned to Jaxson. "What do you think?"

He shrugged. "She's under a lot of stress. It could mean

the owner's husband had blond curly hair, or it could mean nothing."

He wasn't any help. I stood. "It could also mean the thief had that kind of hair. I'm going to see if Steve will tell me anything."

"Seriously?"

"What's the worst that can happen? He'll tell me to go home."

"I guess. Good luck."

Before Iggy could beg to go with me, I headed out. Pearl's replacement, Jennifer Larson, was manning the desk. "Is the sheriff here? It's about the Holt heist."

"Just a moment." She called him, and I held my breath. He might be too stressed to deal with me. Jennifer hung up. "You can go on back."

Phew. When I entered his office, Steve was typing something on his computer. And here I thought he mostly dealt with his yellow legal pad. He looked up. "Have a seat, Glinda."

He sounded unusually professional, a sure sign he was under a lot of pressure.

"I was wondering if you have any news on Mr. Tillman?" I asked.

"Who?"

"The dead man found on the beach today." Why was he playing dumb with me?

"How do you know his name? He had no identification on him."

My pulse shot up at the fact I knew something he didn't. "He was Rihanna's photojournalism teacher at the high school."

No surprise, Steve pulled out his pad. "She never told us. Do you know his first name?"

"No."

"What else do you know about him?"

"Honestly, not much. He came to Witch's Cove shortly before school started, but I don't know from where." I explained a little about his background and how he'd taken photos all over the world.

"Interesting."

Now that I'd given him a piece of information, I hoped he'd reciprocate. "I heard he died from being tasered."

His eyes widened, probably from trying to figure out where the leak came from, especially since his grandmother wasn't at the front desk. "The medical examiner noticed two burn marks on his back, but I won't know more until after the autopsy."

"Thanks."

"Is that all?" he asked.

"Actually, Mrs. Holt came to me and asked if I'd use my knowledge of witchcraft to find her mother's necklace."

"And did you?"

Wouldn't I have acted a bit more excited if I had? "No." I explained about handing the scarf to Gertrude who received the impression of a river. "When Rihanna inadvertently touched it, she had a vision of a man with blond curly hair."

He sat up straighter. "Did she see his face?"

I couldn't believe he didn't dismiss the witchcraft part. "No. She only saw the back of the man's head. It shook her. I don't think she expected to get any kind of reading from the scarf."

"I see. Anything else?"

"Were you aware that a house in Palm Ridge had been broken into about a week ago? The owner had stuff taken from her safe, too. The odd part was that the thief was able to get in and out without breaking any windows. And get this, the doors were all locked."

"That sounds very much like the Holt case. I'll give Sheriff Dunfield from Palm Ridge a call."

"Great. If this person hit two places successfully, he may hit again."

"I'll contact a few of the surrounding sheriffs to see if they have something similar. If nothing else, they should be warned." He leaned back in his chair, acting as if he didn't have a care in the world. "What's your take on the thief?"

He wanted my advice? Cool. "Do you remember when I was able to cloak myself?"

His faced paled. "Don't tell me you think some witch did this?"

"I have a lot of theories, but none are substantiated. Even if this thief could get in and out while managing to lock the door when he left, how did he know the combination to the safe?" I held up my hand. "Again, many theories. Since the MO was the same for the two heists, for now, I'm discounting an inside job."

"That's reasonable."

"Do you know what kind of safe the homeowner had? That is, did it have a dial or was it like those in hotel rooms where you key in four digits?" I didn't want to consider a fancy biometric safe or one that required a key in addition to a code. That would be almost impossible to get into—or so I believed.

"The Holts had a dial safe."

"I'll have to do some research. I know nothing about safe cracking."

He smiled. "Good."

Actually, I'd ask Jaxson to look into it. If I had really valuable items, I'd either keep them in a safety deposit box or buy a safe that required my fingerprint or eye scan to open it.

"Any other theories?" he asked.

I explained about the thief possibly cloaking himself and watching the owner as he opened the safe. "I need to find out how often the Holts accessed their safe."

"Sounds good. How about you explore your paranormal angle, and I'll stick to good old-fashioned detecting."

I couldn't tell if he was being disrespectful or not, but I didn't care. As far as I was concerned, he'd just given me permission to snoop. I just hoped Gertrude would pull through in learning who could open doors with their minds.

I pushed back my chair. "Keep in touch," I said, even though I knew he wouldn't. I hoped that Pearl would return soon. Being cut off from the sheriff's investigation was hurting my business.

I went back to the office, not sure what my next step was going to be. Jaxson turned around. "I think I found something."

My slight depression lifted. I pulled over my chair and sat next to him. "Show me."

"I was looking at the news in the neighboring towns, and I found a few more burglaries that matched the description of the other two break-ins."

"Don't tell me the thief only took stuff from a safe and was able to get in and out without messing with the locks?"

"I don't know about the locks, exactly, but yes, the only items stolen had been taken from a safe."

"Do you have the dates?"

"I do. And the locations. I suppose you'll want to draw a map and color code everything?"

Colors made seeing the patterns easier. "I do, but I'm thinking Rihanna is better suited for the job. She told me she is quite competent using Photoshop."

"I'm not surprised. How about asking her?" Jaxson suggested.

I could have drawn the map by hand, but I thought Rihanna needed something to keep her busy.

I knocked on her door.

"Come in."

If I asked how she was holding up, she'd say fine. "Do you think you can help us with something?"

"What?"

"I need your Photoshop skills."

She sat up, a small light shining in her eyes. "Sure."

Rihanna grabbed her laptop and carried it to the main room where I explained what we needed. "We're looking for a pattern, so maybe put a colored label for the day, one for the time of the heist, and one for the location. Can you do that?"

"Easy peasy."

Jaxson fed her the information. When I studied the result, I couldn't believe the similarity between the thefts. One occurred south of here in Palm Ridge, two to the north in

Ocean View, and two to the east in Summertime. "It seems as if he might not be done. We've only had one in Witch's Cove so far."

Jaxson pointed to the dates. "He robs a home approximately every five days."

"Interesting. Did the articles ever mention a getaway car or anyone seeing someone fleeing the scene?" I asked.

"No."

"It does seem as if the guy is fairly local. So far, he's kept to only four towns."

Jaxson blew out a breath. "The question is whether we will be next or not."

"I say we try to find him before he has the chance to commit another crime."

Chapter Five

ALL LAST NIGHT, Jaxson and I worked on a plan that involved canvasing the neighborhoods where all the thefts had occurred. However, we thought it best not to speak with the homeowners who'd been robbed since we believed that would attract too much attention from the local sheriff. If our escapades got back to Steve, it might create some ill will, something I wanted to avoid, if possible.

We also decided not to check the pawn shops for the stolen goods. That would have been the first thing the cops would have done. We were here to see if my hunch of an invisible thief had any validity.

After we made sure that Rihanna was under the watchful eye of my mother, Jaxson and I drove to Summertime, the town directly east of Witch's Cover. The first address took us to a fairly upscale neighborhood, but that didn't surprise me. I didn't own a safe because I owned nothing of value. I bet these people did.

After Jaxson parked, we walked up and down the street, hoping to spot a house with security cameras, but we didn't find any. If someone had installed some, they were well hidden.

"We have to knock on someone's door," I said.

"Let's see if the neighbor across the street from the place that was robbed is home," he said. "If by some chance they were looking out the window at the time of the theft, they'd have the best view."

It was a long shot, but we'd come all this way, and I wanted to make some progress in the case. Unfortunately, no one answered, which was disappointing since it was a Sunday, and I thought people would be home. It wasn't until the fourth home that we found someone.

"Yes?" It was an elderly woman with kind eyes.

I introduced us and handed the woman our card. When she squinted, I tried not to show my disappointment at her poor eyesight. "We were wondering if by any chance you saw anything the day the Armwoods were robbed?"

"See anything? No, dear, but I heard something. Would you like to come in?"

That sounded promising. "Thank you."

"Who is it?" a man's voice called from another room.

"Some detectives."

We weren't detectives, but why correct her? An elderly gentleman with a cane hobbled out. "You don't look like the law."

Was it because we weren't wearing uniforms, or because we were rather young—at least in his eyes? "We're not. We're sleuths, trying to learn something about the Armwood robbery that happened a week or so ago. It might be connected to a case in our town of Witch's Cove."

"Another robbery? Oh, my goodness. Have a seat." He waved his free hand. "My wife thinks she saw, or maybe it was that she heard something, but she often imagines things."

"I do not." The older woman turned back to us. "Can I get you something to drink?"

"No, thank you." Jaxson and I sat next to each other on the sofa. "What did you see exactly or rather hear?" I asked.

The couple sat on the settee across from us.

"I was doing my dishes, like I do every day after lunch. Mind you, my kitchen window overlooks the street. Then something strange happened."

"Strange? What did you see?"

"A ghost."

The woman's husband waved a hand. "What did I tell you? My wife hasn't been right for a while."

I wasn't so sure about that. "I want to hear what your wife thinks."

She glared at him. "See, Clive. Not everyone believes I'm losing it."

"Go on," I urged. This could be what I thought might have happened.

"I *heard* a door open and then close."

"Did someone come out of the house?" I asked.

"I didn't think so. At least not at first."

Maybe she wasn't of sound mine. "Did they appear out of thin air then?"

She leaned forward. "Yes! Yes!" She turned to Clive. "See? I'm not crazy."

"Sure, dear," he said, clearly not believing her. It was his loss.

"Then what?" I asked.

"Like I said, first, the front door opened. Then the door closed, but I didn't see anyone. That's why I thought it must have been a ghost. A few seconds later, something flickered."

"Flickered?"

"I thought I saw a man wearing a backpack, but he disappeared right before my eyes. Poof."

His ability to hold his cloaking might have failed. "Did you see him a second time?"

"No. Just that once."

"Did you notice any cars driving away?" Jaxson asked.

She looked confused. "A car? I don't think so, but I was still trying to figure out how I could see something one second and then not see him again. I wasn't paying attention to the traffic."

I didn't think it would be good for her mental state if I explained it. "That was very helpful."

"It was?" she asked.

"Yes. More than you can know."

She beamed. Jaxson and I stood and thanked both her and her husband again. When we were outside, Jaxson turned to me. "Do you think it was a warlock?"

"That would be my guess. The door opening implies someone exited," I said. "That's assuming the old lady wasn't losing her mind."

"Suppose she's not. How does that help us?" he asked.

"I'm not sure, but Gertrude is looking into who might be able to open locks with their minds. If she finds this person, I'll ask if he can cloak himself."

"If he is the thief, he won't admit to that talent."

"You're probably right."

When we returned to the car, Jaxson started the engine and took off. "I don't really see the need to find other neighbors. That lady was a goldmine," he said.

"I totally agree. I imagine there will be no witnesses to any of the crimes if the thief was basically invisible."

"That doesn't tell us how he got in or knew the combination to the safe," Jaxson said.

"I know. Entering and leaving without a trace could be magic, but knowing the combination to a safe? That would be supernatural."

He chuckled. "Very true. How about if you ask Mrs. Holt how often they opened their safe? That might help narrow things down."

I had planned to ask her, but then had forgotten. I gave her a call, but her answer wasn't what I wanted to hear. I disconnected. "Neither she nor her husband had opened the safe in the two weeks prior to the break-in," I said.

"I guess that eliminates our warlock following the husband inside and taking note of the combination," Jaxson said as he came to the end of the subdivision.

"Could this person work for a safe company?" I asked.

"Maybe, but that would imply all of the homes had the same brand of safe."

The probability of that was slim, but it was all we had to go on. "We'll have to let Steve know what we found out."

"Assuming he believes us—or rather the neighbor."

"True."

When we arrived in Witch's Cove, Jaxson parked in front of the station. He had the list of homes that had been burgled, as well as the time and day of the theft. "Let's hope he is willing to follow up on these leads," I said.

Inside, Jennifer was still at the reception desk. Because

Steve was in the main area talking to Nash, he saw us and came over.

"Back so soon?"

"We have some information on the burglaries we thought you'd like to know about."

"By all means come to my office."

Jaxson and I took seats in front of Steve's desk as he dropped down behind it. "What did you find?" he asked.

Jaxson handed him the list. "By searching the news feeds from the neighboring towns, I found these other robberies that appeared similar to the Holt case."

Steve pulled open his drawer and yanked out his yellow pad. He flipped to another page and seemed to be comparing them. "Yup. That's what I have."

I was glad to see he was on top of things. "We spoke to a neighbor in Summertime who saw something."

His brows rose. "What was that?"

I described the woman's age and her husband's opinion of her. "Regardless, I believe that she saw the thief leave the house, or rather kind of saw the thief, because he flickered."

"Flickered, as in he was able to disappear like you did?"

Thankfully, he was able to connect the dots. "Yes, but since it's hard to remain invisible, the flickering could have been him reappearing and then immediately recloaking himself."

"Let's assume that's true, how does that help us identify him?" Steve asked.

"It doesn't really, other than we need to be looking for a warlock. I have my feelers out for who that might be."

"Then I'm glad you're on the case."

He was being nice. "Thank you."

"We have another idea," Jaxson said. "But we need your help."

"What's that?"

"Do you know what brand of safe was in each of the burgled homes?"

Steve ran his finger down the list. "No, but I can find out. Why?"

"This might be a long shot, but what if the thief worked for the company that installed the safes? He'd know which homes had them," Jaxson offered.

"Good point. Let me check that out." His cell rang, and he looked at the caller ID. "That's Sheriff Dunfield. I'll only be a sec. I will ask him for the brand of the safe in the Palm Ridge robbery." He swiped a finger. "Don, how can I help you?"

"Another break-in….Oh, no. How is he?" He looked up at us, his eyes full of sympathy. Steve listened for a minute. "I see. Let me know what your M.E. finds out. Thanks." He disconnected.

M.E.? "Was someone else murdered?" I asked.

"Yes, but the man who died isn't in my jurisdiction, so please stay out of it."

"This could change our idea about who might have stolen Mrs. Holt's necklace and her other items."

"I don't see how, but I'll tell you this much. The man's house in Palm Ridge was apparently being burgled at the time of his death. The sheriff suspects the owner walked in on the thief. He says *suspected*, because when neighbors noticed the front door was open, they went inside and found the man face down on the floor with the safe open."

"That's tragic. I don't suppose he lived long enough to give this neighbor a description of the burglar?"

"No."

"That does sound like the thief was interrupted." I was stating the obvious.

"Yes, but here's the strange part. The dead man was tasered. From behind."

"The same way Mr. Tillman died—or so we believe." I tried to create the scene in my mind. "That almost means the thief had an accomplice unless the thief fought with the homeowner and tasered him in the process."

"That would be my guess too, but the medical examiner should be able to tell by the angle of the taser how he died. It's possible the homeowner could have been killed during the struggle, or maybe a second man came up behind him."

"Do you think that Mr. Tillman's death is somehow related to this seeing how they were both tasered in the back?" I looked over at Jaxson to see his reaction. He just lifted a shoulder.

"We'll know more when their M.E. sends over the report. I'll have Dr. Sanchez share her findings too. I don't know a lot about that kind of thing, but I imagine a professional could tell if the two charges were identical."

"That would be great. By any chance, did you find out where Mr. Tillman lived?" I asked Steve.

"The school gave me his address. Why?"

"Maybe he interrupted a thief and was killed because of it. Though why would he be dragged to the beach, while the other man was left in his house?"

"Mr. Tillman doesn't seem to have interrupted a robbery. Nash and I have looked inside his condo. There was no safe, and nothing was disturbed."

Then what happened? "To save you some time, how about if Jaxson and I check out his place?"

"There's nothing to check out, and besides, I don't want you involved."

"I'll take Rihanna with me. She might be able to spot something we can't. She does have some special powers."

He was aware of her ability to hear voices—at least that one time—and to see something when she touched an item, though even I had to admit it could have been a one-time event.

He scribbled something down on paper and slid it across his desk. It was an address. "I can't allow two civilians to get involved. Do you hear me? Let *me* check it out," he announced in a voice loud enough for anyone on the street to hear.

That wasn't obvious or anything. "Of course."

I slipped the paper in my purse without looking at it. Telling us not to get involved and then giving us the address was his way of covering his butt. I could appreciate that.

"You'll need this too." He opened his drawer, extracted a key, and handed it to me.

I figured it was the key to Mr. Tillman's apartment, which was probably also highly illegal. Steve was sticking his neck out for us, and I would do everything I could not to let him down.

I picked it up, waved it, and mouthed a thank you. "You said there was no identification on the victim? No wallet or phone?"

"No. Just his apartment key in his top shirt pocket."

"The thieves might have only cared about money or a phone that they could pawn, unless…"

"Unless what?" Steve asked.

"Mr. Tillman was a photojournalist. Maybe the phone had pictures on it that someone didn't want to get out."

"That is possible."

But we would never see them. "I hope you find the guy who did this to him," I said in a rather loud voice.

"I'm sure we will."

I wanted to remind him to ask Sheriff Dunfield about the brand of safe used in the home that was burglarized, since he hadn't mentioned it during their brief phone call, but I was sure Steve would find out when he had time.

Jaxson and I left. With a hand to my back, he guided me next door to the coffee shop. "We need to discuss our plan before we tell Rihanna anything. My treat."

"You are so sweet."

He grinned. "I try. If Miriam wants to chat, we can't tell her about the new dead body though. Deal?"

I nodded. "Deal. As much as I think reciprocating gossip is needed in our line of work, I don't want to break Steve's confidence. He's already sticking his neck out by giving us the address and the key."

"True."

Inside, we sat at my usual table near the front. Someone other than Miriam came over, for which I was glad. I ordered an iced tea, but this time, I opted for not having anything sweet. Jaxson asked for a black coffee.

"What are you going to tell Rihanna?" he asked.

"I'm thinking the truth. If I try to hide anything, she'll know. I don't want to lose the trust we have built."

"You are one smart woman, Glinda Goodall."

I wasn't so sure of that. "I'm trying."

Chapter Six

"YOU THINK MR. Tillman was killed by some random robbers?" Rihanna asked.

"We honestly don't know," I said. "The other man who was tasered like Mr. Tillman also died. However, he was found at his house. We won't know if the two were killed with the same weapon until the autopsies are compared."

Rihanna leaned back against the sofa at the office. "What are you going to do now?"

"I have Mr. Tillman's home address. I thought the three of us could check out his place to see if there's something there to give us a clue as to who might have killed him—assuming it was premeditated."

"What are you hoping to find?" she asked.

I went through the concept that Mr. Tillman might have taken some photos that someone didn't want seen.

She shook her head. "He wouldn't have blackmailed anyone."

I appreciated that she really liked the guy, but she wasn't being totally objective. "Why do you think that?"

"He told us his photos were of local people living their lives. Nothing more."

"That doesn't mean he didn't inadvertently catch someone on camera who didn't want to be seen."

She nodded. "It's possible, I guess. When we go, do you want me to touch something of his so maybe I'll get a vision about where these incriminating photos are?"

"That would be great if you could, but I'm not holding my breath."

"If Mr. Tillman took photos that someone didn't want to get out, I imagine the thief would have taken them already," Jaxson said.

Thankfully, he didn't add *and then killed him*.

"Maybe, maybe not. The sheriff said the condo didn't look disturbed. They could still be there."

"Then let's check it out," Jaxson said.

"On the other hand," I said second-guessing myself, "I only use my phone when taking my pictures, and we know his phone wasn't on him."

"This little trip might reveal nothing, but I say we look just in case," Jaxson tossed out.

Rihanna nodded. "I agree."

"Then it's settled," I added.

Iggy wanted to come, which I thought was a good idea, since he was able to crawl into small spaces. Who knows? He might find some hidden gem.

"How far away is his apartment?" Rihanna asked.

"I never looked." I pulled the paper out of my purse. "Seriously?"

"Where is it?" Jaxson asked. I handed him the address. He whistled. "What's a teacher doing living at Beachside Condos?"

Was his real job living off blackmail money? Okay, that

wasn't fair. He could have family money, or he could have won the lottery. "Good question."

"What's wrong?" Rihanna asked.

"It's probably nothing, but he lives in a really nice place. I hadn't expected it, that's all."

Rihanna didn't say if her teacher had mentioned whether his parents were well off or anything, but they certainly could have been.

The trip to the condo only took a minute since it was located down the street. I would have suggested we walk, but Mr. Tillman might have some items we wanted to take back with us so we could study them.

"Do you have a key?" she asked.

"I do." I fished it out to make sure I still had it.

His condo was on the sixth floor of a seven-floor building. Sweet. I opened the door, stepped inside, and whistled. "It looks like he had an interior decorator."

Rihanna smiled. "It's so him. Mr. Tillman had style."

"The place might have come furnished, you know. I can't imagine him having the time to decorate. He just moved here," I said.

The slight drop of Rihanna's shoulders convinced me I needed to keep my mouth shut about all things regarding Mr. Tillman.

"Let's spread out and see what we can find," Jaxson said.

He was always so level-headed. "Rihanna, why don't you see where he kept his cameras. They might be helpful."

"I'll search the living room," Jaxson said. "He should have a laptop somewhere."

I don't know why, but I checked out the kitchen. Unfortunately, I found nothing of interest.

"I can't find his laptop," Jaxson said a minute later.

"Do you think Steve confiscated it to find out why someone might want to have harmed him?"

"We'll ask him."

"Check in the bedroom, too," I suggested.

He smiled. "Good thinking."

Before Jaxson had a chance to move, Rihanna called from another room. "Guys, come in here."

My pulse shot up as I rushed toward her. The last thing I expected to see was her smiling. "What is it?"

"Look at this room? It's so perfect."

I didn't need to ask why, probably because even I thought it looked as if the designer had put it together with Rihanna in mind. The dresser, side table, and bed were made out of a near-black wood. The bedspread was white, and the throw pillows had a cool black and white pattern on them.

Above the bed were several black framed photos of black and white portraits from around the world. If I had to guess, I'd say they had been taken by Mr. Tillman. It would be the perfect Rihanna Samuels' room.

"This is beautiful," I admitted. "Did you find anything in the drawers? Maybe he had a child."

She shook her head. "I didn't look, but he said he wasn't married."

That was a rather personal thing to tell his students, but I didn't want to get into it. Even if he wasn't married now, he could have been divorced and had shared custody of his child. "See if you can find his cameras, Rihanna."

"Sure."

She slipped out of the room. To make sure I wasn't missing something, I checked the drawers and the closet, but everything was empty. Next, I headed to the other bedroom. If the man had never married, why rent a two-bedroom place—other than what I speculated about joint custody of a child? Then again, it could be just a uniquely decorated guest room.

In the other room, the bed was a mess. That was more like it.

Jaxson faced me. "No computer in here either."

"It could be at school," Rihanna said. "He had one there."

"Good to know. We can ask if maybe Steve can get it from them." When I looked into his closet, I noticed two cameras. "Hey, Rihanna. Can you come here?"

"What is it?"

"What do you make of these?" I pointed to the cameras on the top shelf where I couldn't reach.

She pulled one down and whistled. "This is a Hasselblad."

I was no camera expert. "I guess that means it's a good one?"

"The best, but it's not digital."

"Is there film inside then?"

"I don't know. I don't want to open it and expose the pictures in case there is."

That made sense. "What about the other one?"

"That looks like his Canon 5D Mark IV." When she slipped it off the shelf, she stilled.

As much as I wanted to ask if she was okay, I needed to give her a moment in case she was experiencing a vision. She turned around and placed the camera on the bed, almost as if it unnerved her.

"Did something happen?" I asked.

"I saw him holding a baby."

"Maybe it was a child from some village overseas, and another photographer snapped it of him?"

"I don't think so. The background looked familiar, but the image was too quick for me to be able to describe it."

I wrapped an arm around her shoulders. "It's okay. Is this one digital?"

"Yes."

"Maybe there is a memory card inside."

She sniffled, opened the back, and extracted it. "Can we look at it?"

"I don't see why not. We have to give it to the sheriff first since it would be evidence. When he finds the man's family, they'll probably want it, but I imagine we can look at the photos if there is no incriminating evidence on it."

Jaxson stepped into the room. "I didn't find anything of interest anywhere."

"That's okay. Rihanna found his cameras. They might tell us something. Where's Iggy?" I hadn't heard or seen him.

Hearing his name, he waddled in. "He must have a maid."

"Why do you say that?"

"The floor is clean."

I didn't think that was relevant, but I for one never dismiss anything.

Just as we were leaving, Rihanna stepped over to the closet and touched the dead man's clothes. It was a bit creepy, but maybe she could get a sense of the man.

She spun around and looked at Jaxson. "Did you just say something?"

"No. Why?"

"I heard a voice."

I stilled. "What did it say?"

"I can't really be sure. I just heard words."

"Words like what?" I asked.

"Photos. Clouds. Wrong."

I looked over at Jaxson, hoping he could decipher it. "Any idea what that might mean?"

He shook his head. "Maybe he stored his images in the cloud?"

"Even if he did, we'd have no way of accessing them or knowing which cloud service he used," I said.

"Let's go back to the sheriff's office," Jaxson said. "Maybe Steve will have an idea what all of this means."

The trip was a short one. I had to return the key anyway. As much as I wanted to be the first to look at the photos stored on the flash drive, the sheriff had to be the one to do it.

After being directed back to Steve's office, I slid the key across his desk. "Thank you."

He slipped it into his desk drawer and then looked up at my cousin. "Hello, Rihanna."

"Hi."

"Have a seat." He called Nash to bring in a third chair. "What did you learn?"

"First off, I didn't expect Mr. Tillman to live in such an upscale place," I said.

"I agree, but his family could have had money," Steve said.

"Did you look into the man's background?" I figured he had.

"Yes, but the details are sketchy. He was a photojournalist who had traveled all over the world. What I couldn't find out was who he worked for."

"He said he was a freelance photographer," Rihanna said. "He made his money by selling his articles."

"Good to know." Out came the yellow pad. "Anything in his condo give you a clue as to who might have killed him?"

"No," Jaxson said. "However, his computer is missing. That might mean something."

Steve leaned back in his chair. "We have that. We thought it might contain some pertinent information."

I waited for him to tell me what. Only he didn't. "Well, did it?"

"No."

Jaxson shifted in his seat. "Mind if I have a look? I am rather good at finding things on a computer."

"I can't let it out of the office, but you're welcome to take a look at it in the conference room," Steve said.

"I appreciate it."

"What else did you learn?" Steve asked.

I placed both cameras on his desk. I explained that the larger of the two was a film camera but that I didn't know if there was any film inside. "Here is the flash drive from the second one. There might be something on this."

"Thanks. I'll have the film processed, assuming I can find a place to do it."

"Rihanna learned something." I turned to my cousin, hoping she'd be willing to tell him. When she said nothing, I clasped her hand. "It's your story to tell."

She inhaled. "When I held that film camera, I saw—in my mind—an image of who I believe was a younger version of Mr. Tillman holding a baby."

"A baby?" Steve asked. He looked over at me. "Any idea what that means?"

"No. Whatever it was, I personally don't think it had anything to do with the robbery." I turned to my cousin. "Tell him what you heard."

Not wanting to see Steve's reaction, I kept my focus on Rihanna. "When I touched one of his shirts, three words just came to me: photos, cloud, and wrong," Rihanna said.

Steve scribbled them down. "What do you think they mean?"

"I don't speak with the dead, at least I never have, but maybe he wants to tell me to look at the photos he stored in the cloud."

"That makes sense. And the word *wrong*?"

She shook her head. "Maybe someone did something wrong, and Mr. Tillman found out."

Steve nodded. "That make sense, but without any names, I'm not sure what I can do."

"Did you call the local authorities in the towns surrounding ours and ask about the brand of safe?" Jaxson asked.

"I did. I made a copy for you." He ripped off a sheet from his yellow pad and handed it to Jaxson. "All of the safes were the dial up kind. I also followed up and asked the sheriffs to find out where the owners had bought their safes."

"And?" I had a feeling this might be the breakthrough we'd been waiting for.

"They all came from the same hardware store. Emerson's."

We didn't have an Emerson's in Witch's Cove since we were so small, but Summertime did. "Does Palm Ridge or Ocean View have a branch?"

"Nope, just Summertime."

"I don't suppose you learned the name or names of the people who install safes for them?"

"No, I'm not that fast. It's Sunday and the store was short-staffed today, but I will look into it. I did check out the brand of dial safe they sell online, and I found out that the owners have the ability to change the combination."

"That might discredit my theory that the thief was the safe installer."

"Maybe not," Rihanna said. "I have a suitcase that came with a three-digit dial lock. The factory setting is 0-0-0. I know I was supposed to change it, but I never bothered. I would have had to look on the Internet at a video on how to do it, and I was too lazy."

Rihanna was a teenager. I couldn't imagine an adult would put something valuable in a safe and not take the time to change the code. "I have an idea," I said. "Hang on."

I called Mrs. Holt, and she answered right away. "Glinda, did you find it?" she asked, sounding desperate.

"No, I'm sorry. Not yet, but I have a question for you. Do you know where you purchased your safe?"

"My husband took care of that."

"Okay. Do you know if he changed the combination after the safe was installed?"

"I don't know that either, but he's here. Give me a sec

and I'll ask him." I heard her talking to someone. "Okay. He bought the safe at Emerson's over in Summertime. As for changing the combination from the factory setting, he didn't. He said he got busy and forgot." I could hear the disappointment in her voice.

"That's actually helpful. By any chance, do you remember what the man who installed the safe looked like?"

"We get a lot of workers in here, but I think he was the young man with the pretty blond curly hair. I wouldn't have remembered, except that I remarked on it."

I mentally pumped a fist. "Thank you. I'll let you know if we find anything." I disconnected and turned to everyone. "We may have our first break."

Chapter Seven

"WHAT DID YOU find out?" Steve asked me.

I explained that the Holts hadn't changed the manufactured settings on their safe and that the man who installed it had blond curly hair.

"That confirms Rihanna's image," Steve said.

"Yes." I patted her hand.

Jaxson smiled. "Now all we need to do...or rather what the sheriff in Summertime needs to do, is find some blond man who installs safes for Emerson's."

Steve chuckled. "I'll follow up, too. I don't want him to drop the ball on this. I don't imagine he'll believe a person can have a vision, let alone that it might match Mrs. Holt's memory of some worker who came to her house, no telling how long ago."

"Thank you," I said. Steve was a stand-up guy.

"I'll call Emerson's now and get their employee records, but it might not pan out. If this person is a thief, he may not have provided his real name. Not only that, he might not work there anymore."

I was a bit more optimistic.

Nash knocked on the door and then stuck his head in. "Thought you'd want to know that the sheriff's department over in Ocean View found Joe Tillman's car."

"Great. Where was it?" Steve asked.

"On Magnolia and Sanders Avenue."

Rihanna raised a finger. "That's near one of the robberies in Ocean View."

"How did you know that?" She'd only lived in this area a few weeks and had never been to that town, at least not that I knew of.

"I remember where I put the tags that represented the robberies."

Smart girl. Steve pulled out his drawer and looked at the addresses. "I'll be. There was a robbery on that street the night Tillman died."

That was the only theft that occurred during the evening. I thought the homeowners might work the late shift or else had been out of town. Now, at least, we had some kind of connection between Mr. Tillman and the thieves. Was he involved somehow, or was he an innocent passerby? I didn't want to mention any possibility of wrongdoing in front of Rihanna. She'd have a fit.

"What are they going to do with the car?" Steve asked his deputy.

"As soon as they process it, they'll drive it over here."

"Thanks."

Rihanna twisted toward me. "Do you think I could look at the car when it arrives?"

"I'm not the one to ask." I faced Steve. "If the car has been processed, can Rihanna do her thing?"

"I don't see why not. I'll contact you when it gets here."

"Thanks, and one more thing. Any progress on finding

his relatives?" I asked.

"Not yet. The man was a ghost."

That word had a different connotation to me. "Why do you say that?"

"He had a Virginia driver's license, but the address was bogus."

My mind went in a lot of different directions. "What did the high school have to say? They would have done a background check when they hired him."

"It's Sunday, but I'll call them tomorrow. It is one of the many things on my to-do list. A theft and a murder require a lot of legwork."

"I'm sure they do. In that case, we'll get out of your hair."

"Mind if I stay and look over Mr. Tillman's computer?" Jaxson asked.

"No problem. I'll ask Nash to set you up."

Jaxson turned to me. "I'll see you later?"

"You bet."

As Rihanna and I walked across the street to our office, I was a bit disheartened that my cousin was so quiet. "What are you thinking about?" Not that I couldn't guess.

"How sudden life could be taken from a person. Mr. Tillman was larger than life for me. Then he was gone in the blink of an eye."

"I know. My grandmother died quickly too, though not quite as suddenly. She'd had a heart attack and lingered for a few days."

Once back at the office, Iggy jumped out of my purse. "Next time, how about you let me out?"

Whoops. When we were at the sheriff's office, I'd forgotten about him. It wasn't as if Steve would be afraid of Iggy, so I'm betting he wouldn't have minded. "Next time, I'll ask the sheriff. I'm sure he'll be okay with it, as long as you stay close by."

"Okay. One good thing was that I got to learn all the juicy gossip."

I chuckled. Rihanna headed to her room, and I didn't stop her. She was grieving.

Less than fifteen minutes later, a knock sounded on our door, and my mom popped her head inside. That was a shock. She never just stopped by.

"Mom, what's wrong?" I might not be psychic, but I could see the worry lines on her face.

"Where's Rihanna?"

"In her room. Why?"

She inhaled. "There is something I need to tell you both."

This didn't sound good. "I'll get her."

Once Rihanna and I were seated on the sofa, my mom sat down. "The medical examiner delivered Joe Tillman's body this morning."

"Mom, maybe Rihanna shouldn't be here for this."

She held up a palm. "No, she does." Mom drew in a deep breath. "When I was preparing the body, I noticed a tattoo on his chest—or rather the remnants of a tattoo. He'd tried to get it removed, but the outline of an image remained."

I had no idea why we needed to hear this. "And?"

"I recognized it. It was the three letters LTR, only the last two were done in a scrolly-type font. It was unique. But there is more. I knew this man, or I did sixteen years ago."

I did the math, but I wasn't ready to draw any conclusions. "What are you saying?"

"That Joe Tillman is really Lucas Samuels." Mom turned to Rihanna. "I am so sorry. I had no idea your father hadn't died all these years ago."

Rihanna's face turned white. "You're wrong. My dad died when I was one."

"Hoping I was wrong, I took a photo of his face and sent the picture, along with the faded tattoo to your mom. She confirmed it was him and then confessed everything."

Rihanna was shaking. "I don't understand."

Neither did I, for that matter. I wished Jaxson had been here to help navigate this with me.

"The tattoo stood for Lucas, Tricia, and Rihanna. Hence the LTR. Your mother told us that your father was a warlock, and as such, had many talents. One was that he could hear people's thoughts."

Rihanna's body shook. "Like I heard Mr. Plimpton's thoughts." Her voice faded off.

"Yes."

"What happened to him?" And why did Mom tell me he was dead?"

"I need to give you a little background that I only just learned about. Your father was recruited by a branch of our government. It was some Black Ops organization whose purpose was to root out terrorist cells. They sent your father to some very dangerous places where he went in undercover. He didn't need to say much. He just needed to listen. Mind you, he only heard bits and pieces of what the person was thinking, but it was often enough. After he learned when some malicious event would occur, he'd get the news to his boss and then move on. He had to change his name, his location, and create a whole new identity every time."

"You're saying he became Joe Tillman?" Rihanna asked.

"Yes, but...there is a lot more to the story. When your dad took the job, he had to choose between his wife and newborn daughter and his country. He couldn't have both. That would have put you and your mom in grave danger."

"Why fake his own death?" she asked. "Why not just leave?"

"He couldn't afford to have you and your mom tied to him in any way. The bad people had to believe Lucas Samuels was dead. Before you ask, yes, your mom knew about it. I didn't ask her if she supported the decision, but I'm guessing she didn't have much of a choice. Your father insisted that they divorce right before he disappeared so that she could move on with her life. Without a body, she'd have to wait seven years to claim he was dead."

Rihanna dropped her head in her hands, and I rubbed her back. Pain radiated off her at the betrayal.

She finally lifted her head. "Why didn't she tell me?"

"I asked her that. She said you were such a determined child that you would have asked too many questions—of her and probably of the US government. That, in turn, would have put your life in danger."

"Why didn't he call or something? I was his daughter." Her voice escalated in volume.

Even I could answer that. "Rihanna, calls and messages can be traced. Besides, I bet it was very hard on your dad knowing he had a daughter he couldn't be with. He probably suffered just as much as you did."

"Then why come here now?"

"That I can answer," my mom said. "After twenty years of service, your father retired. Your mom knew he was alive, because every few months she'd find a deposit in her bank account. Lucas, your dad, said he'd send money when he could."

"Did mom get to see him at all?"

"Yes, but the first time was a few weeks ago. He contacted her when you weren't home. He was the one who convinced her to go into rehab."

Tears streamed down her face. "I'm glad for that."

"He wanted to be with you more than anything, but to just walk up to you after all these years and announce he was your father might not have gone over well. It was why he pulled some strings to get a job at the high school where you would be attending. I imagine that once he established a rapport with you, he would let you know his real identity," my mom said.

Rihanna's mouth opened. "Oh my gosh. That's why he told me he wanted to talk to me on Monday." She looked over at me with tears that seemed to sparkle. "I bet it was to tell me the truth."

"I wouldn't be surprised," I said as I had another revelation. "I also wouldn't be surprised if that's why he rented a two-bedroom apartment, one that was decorated in black."

She sniffled. "Do you think it was meant for me?"

"I bet it was."

"I need to call my mom," Rihanna said.

"You go ahead." She must have a lot of questions, ones that she deserved to know the answer to. I looked over at my mother. "I can't believe Uncle Lucas was Joe Tillman. I wished I'd seen him again."

My mom nodded. "Me, too."

Only then did I realize my mother had been the one who had to tell her sister that her husband really had died. "How did Aunt Tricia take the news?"

"How do you expect? She was finally turning her life around, because the one man she loved more than anything had returned. Before they could be together, he was murdered. It's such a tragedy."

"I'm so sorry."

"I know," Mom said. "This is doubly hard for Rihanna. I'm sure she feels betrayed by her mom and her dad."

"And Mr. Tillman. They did have a connection—a strong one—but now her memories of him might be tainted." I sucked in a breath.

"What is it? I know that look, Glinda."

"When Rihanna picked up one of her dad's cameras, she had an image of him holding a baby."

Mom smiled. "That means they are psychically connected."

"Meaning what? You think she'll be able to communicate with him on command?"

"It's a thought, but she'd have to be trained first. I tried to contact Lucas, but he didn't respond."

"Rihanna has been rather resistant to embrace her talents."

"I understand that," my mom said. "It can be scary, but if she knows she might be able to talk to her father, she might change her mind. I know your Aunt Tricia wanted nothing to do with the occult, but I'm betting that Rihanna is quite powerful. If the US government recruited her father, he must have been extraordinary."

"I agree. Did Aunt Tricia know the name of his boss? He might be able to tell us more."

"No. Lucas said the less she knew, the safer she'd be."

Wow. This was really hard to grasp. "What do we do now?"

"I'll ask Tricia to call the sheriff and tell him that Rihanna is Joe Tillman's, aka Lucas Samuels', daughter."

"He might ask for a blood test."

"I can help with that," my mom said.

My mind raced ahead to logistics. It was what helped calm me. "We'll have to decide when to have the viewing."

Mom nodded. "I'll call the school and give them some open dates. Some students and staff might want to attend."

I was happy to have her handle that. "Thanks."

Mom stood and hugged me goodbye. Families could be so fragile. After she left, I knocked on Rihanna's bedroom door. "Hey, hon?"

She opened up. "Yes?"

"Are you up for going back to the sheriff's office? Your dad's car might be there." Just because Steve hadn't called didn't mean the vehicle hadn't arrived. He might have been too busy to contact me. Ocean View was only a few miles away.

"So?"

This was going to be difficult. "I thought you might get a reading off it. Or don't you want to find out who killed him and why?"

She sniffled. "Of course, I do."

"Good." This might help her find closure.

We headed back to the sheriff's office. When I spotted Jaxson in the enclosed glass conference room, I tapped on the window to get his attention. He stepped out of the room. "What's up?"

"A new development. A big one. Come into Steve's office."

I didn't want to blurt out that Mr. Tillman was really Rihanna's dead father.

Once we were seated, I broke the news to both of them.

"You're telling me some retired Black Ops guy comes to Witch's Cove to be reunited with the daughter he hasn't seen in sixteen years only to possibly be killed by some thugs?"

I thought Steve summed it up really well. "Yes."

He whistled. He pulled open his drawer and handed me the key to Uncle Lucas' condo. "I guess you'll be needing this."

I didn't think he would take my word for it, but I was glad he did. "Thanks. I'll let the management know my uncle won't be returning. In the meantime, could Rihanna check out her dad's car if it's here?" It sounded funny saying that Mr. Tillman was her father.

"Sure. The sheriff's department over in Ocean View just delivered it." He opened his drawer again, retrieved a key, and handed it to me. "It's the blue Toyota parked out back."

I figured there was only one with that color and model. "Thanks. I trust the sheriff's department didn't find anything useful in the car?"

"No clues and no pictures."

Finding out who killed my uncle wasn't going to be easy. I turned to Rihanna. "Ready to do this?"

"I think so."

Chapter Eight

RIHANNA SAT IN her father's car for quite some time, while I patiently waited outside for her to sense something. Seeing her despair slowly grow tore at me. I wanted to ask her questions and make suggestions, but I thought she needed to do this at her own pace.

Eventually, her head lowered, and then she slipped out of the front seat.

"So?" I asked, trying to sound supportive.

She shook her head. "It's like this car belonged to a stranger."

"That's okay. We'll figure something out." I wasn't sure if now was a good time to bring up training, but I had to do it sometime. "My mom thinks that since you were able to connect with your father's camera, with a little bit of work, you might be able to talk directly to him."

"Like Aunt Wendy can talk to the dead?"

I shrugged. "I'm not sure if that's exactly what she meant, but how would you like to explore your witch side?" I held up a hand. "I know your mom didn't embrace it, but maybe that was because witchcraft was what took your dad away."

"Can I think about it?"

"Of course. We have a very talented witch right here in

Witch's Cove who can help. Her name is Gertrude Poole. She's old, but she's kind and good. She taught me how to become invisible."

"You can cloak yourself?" Rihanna's eyes widened, and my ego flared.

"Yes, but it takes a lot out of me, and I'm not good at controlling it. The cloaking worked well enough to get the job done though. I think that is what the thieves are doing to get into homes without notice. I haven't figured out how they can manipulate locks, but Gertrude said she might be able to find out."

"That's great. Do you think we can maybe drive by the house that was robbed? The one my dad was parked nearby?" she asked.

"Why?"

"I don't know. I might sense something from it."

"How about if we wait to see if the pictures on the digital camera shed any light on things first?"

Her moodiness surfaced. "I guess."

"Come on. Maybe Jaxson has finished with your dad's computer and found something. We need to give Steve the car keys back anyway."

"Okay."

Inside, I found Jaxson coming out of the sheriff department's conference room. "Well?" I asked.

"I might have found something, but I need to do a little more research."

That was cryptic. "Okay." I waved the car keys. "I'll drop these off with Steve, and then we can see what you found."

I knocked on the sheriff's door. Because he was on the

phone, I placed the keys on his desk. He covered his phone. "Anything?"

"No, but we're not giving up."

He nodded and went back to his conversation. The three of us left and headed back to our office. I couldn't wait to hear what Jaxson found out. "You look excited."

"I found his password to his cloud account. I'm hoping I can access his photos from his computer."

"I often send the photos I take directly to the cloud as a backup," Rihanna said. "Maybe the last pictures he took are there."

I doubted we'd get that lucky, but maybe we would. Inside the office, Jaxson entered my uncle's password into some cloud program.

He turned around. "I'm in!"

Rihanna and I pulled up a chair on either side of him and waited for the photos to load. And waited. "How many does he have?" I asked.

"Probably thousands," Rihanna said.

Once they loaded, Jaxson clicked on the most recent one. "The house is nice, but it doesn't seem like the type of shot he takes," I said, though I was no expert. "I have an idea. Jaxson, what was the address of the last theft?"

He pulled a piece of yellow notepad paper from his pocket. "I see where you're going with this."

He typed the address into the map function and used the little man to walk around the street. "There," I nearly shouted. "It's the same house."

"Was he some private investigator or something?" Rihanna asked.

"I don't know, but I doubt it. Uncle Lucas wasn't in town long enough to get clients—or so I would think. Let's keep looking at the pictures."

Jaxson scrolled through a few more. There was a shot of a partially opened front door, but no person was emerging. The next one was the door closed, but no one was on the stoop either. It was a strange choice of things to take. None had any artistic merit, and the fact it was dark out didn't help either.

Jaxson clicked on the next icon. "This one is a movie," he said.

"The quality is rather good, but I still didn't see any people." Off in the distance, a bike moved and then disappeared. "Did you guys see that?" I asked.

Rihanna leaned forward. "See what?"

"There was a bike visible one second and then gone the next."

"If an invisible person sat on a bike, would it disappear?" she asked.

For once, I could answer with certainty. "Yes."

The movie kept going. All of a sudden, a yelp sounded and then the camera fell to the ground. The image turned black.

"What happened?" Rihanna asked.

"I don't know. Maybe his battery ran out of power." That was a lie. I had the sense it was the moment her father had been tasered. If he had died immediately, he must have an automatic cloud back-up in place.

"That's not true. You think it was when he was tasered and died."

Oh, no. I totally forgot about her ability to sometimes

read minds. "Maybe."

"We should show this to Steve," Jaxson said with controlled composure.

"Show him what? A door opening and closing?"

"The bike disappearing confirms our theory that the thief or thieves are warlocks," Jaxson said.

"I think we've proven that, but sure, show Steve."

"Why would they move my dad's body to the beach?"

I looked over at Jaxson, but he just shrugged. "I'd be guessing, but maybe when they took his wallet, they realized he lived on the beach. They might want his death to have looked like a standard mugging."

"That sounds reasonable," Jaxson said. "Having a body in front of a house I'd just robbed, would draw way too much attention."

Rihanna sighed. "That makes sense."

"The question now is how are we able to identify these men? We can't catch what we can't see," I said.

"Is there a spell you can put on someone to stop them from becoming invisible?" Rihanna asked.

"That's a great question. I would like to know the answer to that myself. However, it's not like it would do much good since we don't know when or where these thieves will strike next."

She smiled. "Maybe I'll get lucky and read someone's mind."

"No," I said without a second thought. "These guys have already killed one or maybe two men. They have nothing to lose by killing someone they think is in their way."

"Not if I'm more powerful than they are." Rihanna lifted

her chin.

"What are you talking about?" I asked.

"My dad survived twenty years against the worst of the worst. He must have had skills besides just being able to read minds. You asked if I'd like to explore my capabilities. I've decided. The answer is yes."

I wasn't sure that was a good idea now, but she had the right to do what she wanted with her life. "On one condition. I come with you."

"Sure. You might pick up some skills, too."

Rihanna implied I needed help, but that was okay. I did. I looked over at Jaxson to see his reaction. "What do you think?"

"You trust Gertrude. I say give it a try. The more powerful you both are, the better able you'll be to protect yourselves."

He was right. "Thank you." I checked my watch. "It's probably too late to see Gertrude now, but I'll call tomorrow to make an appointment."

"Okay," Rihanna said.

"I'll send these photos and this movie over to Steve with an explanation of what I think it means," Jaxson said.

"Perfect." I turned to Rihanna. "I'm not sure when your dad's memorial will be, but the service should be soon. My mom likes to display a photo of the person who's passed. If you email her your favorite shot of Mr. Tillman—or rather your dad—she'll have it blown up and mounted."

"I'll do that right now."

"Good. When you're done, how about we grab something to eat and then get some rest? Remember, you have school tomorrow."

She stiffened. "I'm not going to school."

I wasn't sure if I should push it. Her father had just died. "Do you want me to call in and tell them about your dad?"

"Go ahead. Finding my dad's killer is more important than school. I'll even let you help me with my math homework."

She knew how to get to me. "Deal."

EARLY THE NEXT morning, I called in and told them about Rihanna learning that Mr. Tillman was her father. "She just needs a few days to come to grips with this all," I explained to the guidance counselor.

"Of course. We'll email her the homework."

"Thank you."

Next, I made an appointment with Gertrude who said she could see us in an hour. I knocked on Rihanna's bedroom door and told her to get ready.

"What do you think she'll have me do?" my cousin asked as she slipped out of bed.

"I have no idea, but I imagine she'll ask what you want to learn first."

"Okay. I'll think about it."

I loved how calm she appeared. I wasn't that confident in high school. When it was time to go, we walked over to the Psychics Corner. No surprise, Iggy asked if he could come.

"It will be boring," I warned.

"No, it won't. Gertrude and I go way back."

I laughed. He'd visited her one time, but they had interacted at the house a couple of times. "Sure then. Hop in my purse. But this is Rihanna's time. Gertrude is not there to train you."

"You think she could teach me to read minds? That would be so cool."

"No." What had I started? I pressed on his head to keep him hidden in my purse.

In the lobby of the Psychics Corner, we were told to go back to Gertrude's office. Inside, Gertrude stood and smiled. "Welcome to Witch's Cove," she said to Rihanna.

"Hello, Mrs. Poole," my cousin said.

"Call me Gertrude." She studied my cousin without saying a word.

Rihanna smiled. "Thank you, I would like some...Gertrude."

Rihanna's comment made no sense—at least to me.

"Would you like some tea, too, Glinda?"

"Yes, thank you." I looked over at Rihanna. "Did you just read her mind and answer?"

Rihanna grinned. "I did. I think this room relaxes me and brings out my inner witch."

Iggy crawled out of my purse and looked up at me. "May I have some water?" he asked Gertrude.

"Of course. So glad you could join us, Detective Iggy."

Had she read the name on his collar that quickly? I wouldn't be surprised if she just knew. Gertrude was highly talented.

Once she served us drinks, we sat down. Gertrude looked over at Rihanna. "You want to improve your mind reading skills, correct?"

I hadn't said anything about why we wanted to come here.

"I do."

Gertrude sipped her tea. "Here's the thing. There are a lot of hurdles to doing this. Sure, the person whose mind you want to read needs to be receptive, but you have to be willing to listen."

Rihanna looked over at me and then back at Gertrude. "Is there a technique I need to use?"

"I've known Glinda for a long time, and from the way you dress, the two of you are quite alike."

We both looked at each other. "I look nothing like Glinda. She only wears pink. I hate pink," Rihanna said.

Gertrude smiled. "And you only wear black. Am I right?"

"Yes. So?"

I might have commented on her snippy attitude, but I wasn't her mother.

"Both of you are too rigid. If you want to read minds, you can't make the people around you uncomfortable. You need to blend in," Gertrude said. "That being said, start with something small."

"Meaning what?" Rihanna's tone did not soften.

"Change your lipstick or eyeshadow color. In a few days, change a little bit more. Maybe add a white scarf, or go really bold and wear a white shirt—or any color other than black."

"Me, wear white?"

"Why not? Your powers, Rihanna, are being held in by your rigid exterior. I understand that the only way for you to have any kind of control in your life is to choose what to wear.

You don't want anyone to tell you how to lead your life."

Rihanna looked down at her hands. "I guess so."

Wow. Was I doing that? I didn't think so. I had two loving parents, and my life was good. To show solidarity, I suppose I could wear a different colored scarf or maybe even a pink shirt that was trimmed in green. I shivered at that thought.

"We can do a little shopping this afternoon and see how far we can get out of our comfort zone." I wanted to be supportive.

Rihanna's lips pressed together, but then she nodded. "I'll try."

"Good," Gertrude said. "Let's hold hands and close our eyes. I want to try something."

We did as she asked. I thought Gertrude would continue with the instructions, but she said nothing. I was tempted to see what was going on, but I figured this might be some kind of test.

"Hot."

The word jumped into my head from nowhere. The odd thing was that I was not hot, so why would I think that?

"Kind. Good."

I was beginning to get creeped out here. I swear I wasn't thinking those thoughts. Were they coming from Gertrude? Or Rihanna? Or some other place? I couldn't read minds, so what was going on?

Gertrude released her hold on my hand. "Open your eyes, ladies."

We did. I waited for Rihanna to say something, but she just sat there. "Okay, I'll say it. I know this exercise was for my cousin, but I heard words."

"What kind of words?" Gertrude asked.

"I heard *hot, kind,* and *good.*"

Rihanna grinned. "So did I!"

Gertrude leaned back in her chair. "Excellent ladies. I'm glad that the messages were received."

"You sent them?" I asked.

"I did."

Rihanna let go of my hand. "I heard more."

"I imagine you would have. Glinda mentioned that your father was very talented in that department."

"He was, or so I've been told."

"Let's see how we can further sharpen your skills then."

Chapter Nine

WHEN WE LEFT Gertrude's office, my mind was spinning, and Rihanna was positively glowing. "That was incredible," she said.

"You did really well. Are you willing to do a little shopping to see if changing a few things can help our powers of perception?"

"I guess, but hearing Gertrude's voice in my head was unsettling."

"I know, and I only heard three words." She pressed her lips together. "We don't have to do this, if you don't want to."

Rihanna shook her head. "No. I have to. For my dad. I need to find out why he was at that house, and I don't think it was to steal stuff from some random safe. I want those who did this caught."

"Me, too. To be honest, if warlocks are involved, we might be the only ones who can help."

Rihanna inhaled deeply and then nodded.

After I dropped Iggy back at the office, we headed to a very kitschy clothing store that I've always loved. The hard part would be choosing something that wasn't pink. When we entered, Rihanna went straight to the clothes that were black. This might be harder than I thought.

Being the elder of the two, I had to overcome my issues. I found a cute blouse that was green trimmed in pink. That was a definite start. I personally didn't think I needed to change my makeup, but I was willing to take out the pink hair extensions. I already had painted the tips of my nails black when Rihanna first arrived to show support.

Keeping an open mind, I tried on the shirt and found I actually liked the look of it. When I stepped back into the showroom, Rihanna hadn't picked out anything. She was definitely struggling. "No luck?" I asked.

"This is impossible."

"No, it's not. Think of your dad," I said in my mind. She'd read my thoughts before. Maybe she could do it again.

Rihanna smiled. "Good ploy."

I guess that meant she understood, which was a bit frightening to have someone that powerful around me.

Eventually, Rihanna bought a light blue scarf and some matching blue dangling earrings. We decided to wear our purchases out so we could test Gertrude's theory that stepping out of our comfort zone would help with our magical abilities.

"I say we celebrate our new adventure at the ice cream shop."

She smiled. "Sounds great."

My hope was that while we were enjoying our treat, Rihanna might pick up a bit of local chatter. I honestly didn't understand this mind reading stuff, but I wanted to encourage her.

While standing at the ice cream counter, I was about to order my usual scoop of mint chocolate chip, when I decided to mix it up with chocolate chip cookie dough ice cream.

Somehow, Rihanna seemed to understand.

"I really want an ice cream sundae, but I'll take a scoop of the lemon ice instead."

Changing our attire, even a little, might have been a good suggestion on Gertrude's part. Once we had our sweets, we decided to sit outside since most of the customers were out there. The shop also had a nice awning that blocked most of the sun.

I wanted to keep quiet for a bit so that Rihanna could listen. She'd nod every once in a while. She then laughed and quickly covered her mouth.

"What did you hear?" I whispered.

"Of course, we can't help but hear those two girls chat," she said, "but there is a boy at the table next to them. He thinks the brunette is being a jerk. I have to agree."

I had to check them out. Two teen girls were at one table, and a lone boy was at the next one. "You could hear what he was thinking?" That was highly impressive.

"Not full thoughts. But yes."

"Maybe I should go full on black and see what I can pick up." I was hearing nothing but cars going by and the two chatty girls talking about someone at school.

Rihanna smiled. "I'd like to see that."

"Yeah, no. Baby steps."

"Me, too."

"When we finish here, what do you say we stop by the funeral home to see if my mom has made any progress on scheduling the service or in contacting Uncle Lucas."

"I thought you said she'd tried talking to him already, but they didn't connect."

"It usually takes time for the deceased to talk, but he might have decided it was time to say something," I told her.

"Oh, okay."

She sounded forlorn. "What's wrong?"

"I kind of wanted to be the first to talk to him."

I could understand that. "Then I won't suggest to Mom that she try again."

"Thank you."

After we finished, we walked back over to the funeral home. When we entered—from the main entrance this time—Rihanna smiled as she walked on the yellow runner. It was another one of my mom's tributes to the movie, *The Wizard of Oz.*

"I bet she's in the viewing room," I said.

We stepped inside and found her at the end of the room adjusting a photo on an easel that held an enlarged image of Rihanna's dad. It looked so good.

"How did she get it enlarged so quickly?" Rihanna asked.

"Mom works with a shop that does custom work. They are fast."

"It looks nice." Rihanna grabbed my hand and squeezed.

I didn't need to be psychic to understand the overwhelming emotions coursing through her. "It sure does."

She leaned closer. "Your mom is almost in tears."

I didn't see any evidence, but I trusted Rihanna to have sensed it. "I imagine she would be. She never had the chance to talk to your dad again."

We met up with her. "Hey, Mom. The photo looks great!"

"It does. Rihanna, you did such a nice job."

"Thank you."

"Do you have a time and date for the viewing?" I asked.

"Yes. It's tomorrow night at seven."

"So soon?"

"There's really no need to wait." Only then did my mother notice our new attire. "What's going on, girls? Glinda, green? Really? This isn't like you."

I explained what Gertrude said about us needing to get out of our comfort zone.

"I hope it works."

"So do I."

Rihanna turned to me. "I'd like to head back and do some homework. If the service is tomorrow, I want to be at school to make sure all the kids in my photo class know about it."

"That's a great idea." Being around friends might help take her mind off of her loss.

When we returned to the office, Jaxson wasn't there. "Iggy, do you know where Jaxson is?" He hadn't been there when we'd dropped Iggy off either.

"No."

"Thanks."

Rihanna went into her bedroom, and I sat on the sofa, trying to figure out my next move. I thought the consultation with Gertrude went better than expected, and I couldn't wait until the next time to see what was in store for us.

Before I could figure out how to proceed, Jaxson rushed inside. "Oh," he said. "I thought you and Rihanna were out."

He stood there in a T-shirt that was soaked in sweat. "We just got back. What have you been doing?"

"I signed up for a martial art class at the gym."

"Why?"

He chuckled. "Why not? Honestly, I want to be able to protect you and Rihanna. If we're going to be in the business of finding out who murdered people or who stole something, we're bound to upset someone."

All I could do was stare at his sculptured chest. "That sounds great."

Can I just say how glad I was that he couldn't read my mind?

"I need to shower. Is Rihanna in her room?"

"She is." Because we didn't know when we'd need to change, Jaxson kept a spare set of clothes in the bathroom. His house was a bit too far to drive to on a moment's notice.

"Nice shirt, by the way." He winked and strode toward the bathroom.

Nice shirt? That's all? I thought he'd question my sanity. I had to admit, he looked pleased. Interesting.

The shower turned on, and I tried to keep my imagination from going wild.

LET ME SAY upfront: I don't like viewings. Especially when it's someone I knew. I had to be at the memorial service, though, to support Rihanna. We'd thought my Uncle Lucas had died back when I was only ten, so to be honest, I barely remembered him.

Rihanna and I were seated in contemplative silence, waiting for more of her classmates to arrive and for the eulogy to begin. As I checked out who was already there, I couldn't tell who was a witch, a warlock, or neither, but that didn't mean others more talented than me didn't know. If Mr. Tillman—Lucas Samuels—was as powerful as I was led to believe, someone might have known about his abilities and wanted to silence him.

Why did it matter now? It was possible the killer wanted to make sure my uncle was dead. The big question was whether this person would come to the viewing?

When most of the seats were full, the preacher my mom had invited gave a eulogy, even though he'd never met Rihanna's dad. After he finished, he looked around the audience. "Would anyone else like to say a few words?"

I looked over at Rihanna. "Go on up."

Wearing her new white shirt, she stepped up to the podium. "I didn't get to know my dad until the last week of his life."

The crowd rumbled. Her speech was impassioned and very moving. After that, I certainly wasn't going to speak. Even if I did, I didn't know what I'd say.

As Rihanna was walking back to her seat, she stopped in mid stride. "Mom?"

I spun around. I couldn't believe Aunt Tricia had been able to come, though most likely my mom had something to do with it. Rihanna ran to her mother, and the two women hugged. I couldn't hear what they said to each other, but that was okay. Their conversation should be private.

With shimmering eyes, Rihanna returned to her seat as her mother walked up to the podium. I grabbed Rihanna's hand and squeezed. This had to be very hard for both her and my aunt. I didn't say anything, hoping Rihanna could tell what I was thinking—that I was very proud of her.

"Lucas Samuels was my husband—at least he was for two years. He then disappeared off the face of the Earth."

People leaned over to whisper to the person next to them. I couldn't blame them. The story was quite strange and spellbinding. After Aunt Tricia finished her tale of how dedicated Lucas Samuels was to our country, people stood and mingled. A few walked by the open coffin, but I didn't have the heart to.

Rihanna squeezed my leg. "That's him."

"That's who?"

"See the man with the blond curly hair peering down at my dad?"

There were a lot of people with rather unruly looking dirty blond hair, but only one was at the coffin. "You mean the one in the blue jeans and black shirt?"

"Yes."

"You don't think he's the warlock who...?" I couldn't even finish my question.

"I'm sure of it. He's thinking that he's glad my dad is dead."

How had she been able to hear a whole sentence, let alone focus just on him?

Regardless of how, I wanted to call Steve right now, only we didn't have any tangible proof this was the killer. Just then Jaxson came in and slipped in next to us. He'd told me he would be late, since he had something that he needed to take care of. "How did it go?" he said in a low voice.

"The speeches went well. See the man who is now walking away from the coffin?"

"The guy in blue jeans?"

"Yes. Rihanna thinks he is the man who killed her father."

He twisted toward me. "How does she know?"

A click sounded to my left. She'd taken a picture of him. "Rihanna. You can't let him see you." I couldn't help but whisper a strong warning to her.

"Maybe I want to remember who came? He won't think anything of it."

She was being naïve. "Who's to say he can't read minds, too?"

Her mouth dropped open. "That's not good."

"No, it's not."

Jaxson leaned close to me. "Can she tell if he is a you-know-what?"

I'm guessing he wasn't comfortable labeling him a war-lock out loud.

"I don't know."

Rihanna stood. "I want to talk to him."

I grabbed her wrist. "Please. Don't. If he's our man, we'll find something to tie him to your dad's murder."

"Glinda is right, Rihanna. It won't do any good other than to put a target on your back."

She sat back down. "I guess."

The blond man in question mingled a bit and then left, passing her mom and my mom who were in a deep conversation.

Rihanna nudged me. "Oh, look. Gavin came."

The joy in her voice was such a relief. I could only hope she'd abandon her desire to find this blond man. "How nice of him. Why don't you talk to him?"

"And say what?"

"Thank him for coming. You could even ask how he's holding up. I bet working with his mom can't be easy."

She nodded. "That's a good idea."

Fingers crossed, Gavin could help her through this trying time.

Chapter Ten

JAXSON REACHED OUT and clasped my hand. "How are you doing?"

"Me? Fine. I'm just worried about Rihanna."

"I know, but I bet your mom and aunt are upset, too. Your mother knew her brother-in-law, even if it was for a short time. I can't imagine what your aunt must be going through."

He was right. Everyone around me was grieving, not just my cousin.

"Glinda?"

I looked up. "Penny!"

The moment I saw my best friend's face, my worries disappeared for a moment. Jaxson stood and escorted me to the end of the aisle.

She hugged me. "I'm so sorry to hear about your uncle. How are you doing?"

Guilt swamped me for not having kept her in the loop, but things had been crazy of late. Her beau, Hunter Ashwell, was standing next to her with his arm around her waist. "Thanks. I'm good. To be honest. I didn't really know the man."

We talked for a bit more, and only then did I see my

mom in the back talking with Dolly, Maude, and Miriam. Pearl, Steve's grandmother, must still be out of town.

Out of the corner of my eye, I spotted Steve walking in, and I couldn't help but wonder if it was to see who might show. Had he figured out that perhaps the killer wanted to be certain my uncle was indeed dead?

"Can you excuse me for a moment? I want to mention something to our illustrious sheriff."

"Sure."

Jaxson stayed with Penny and Hunter while I made my way over to Steve. Several people I'd waited on numerous times at the Tiki Hut Grill stopped me and offered their condolences. I thanked them for their support. Eventually, I reached Steve.

"I'm sorry about your uncle, Glinda," Steve said.

"Thanks. I wanted to tell you something that Rihanna noticed." I mentioned the blond man and how she'd heard his thoughts.

"I'm not sure what I can do, unless you can give me a name. Then I can keep an eye on him."

"That's the problem. We don't know who he is. Rihanna wants to confront him," I said. "I told her not to, that it was way too dangerous if he is the man who murdered the homeowner and her father."

Steve looked around. "You're right. I'll talk to her if you want. Where is she?"

When I couldn't find her, my stomach did a somersault. "She was just talking to Gavin."

Steve clasped my hand. "Don't worry. I'll locate her."

"Thank you."

He spun around and headed outside. Thank goodness he understood how headstrong Rihanna could be. Jaxson rushed up to me. "Is everything okay?"

"No. Rihanna is missing. Steve is out there looking for her."

"Do you want me to help search?" he asked.

I did, and I didn't. "Can you just stay here with me?"

"Of course." He hugged me, and his warmth seeped into my soul, releasing some of the anxiety coursing through me. Jaxson let go. "Why aren't you rushing out to look for her?"

"I want to, but I don't want to leave my mom or my aunt. I'm hoping Rihanna left to be with Gavin and not because she wanted to follow the guy who she thinks killed her dad."

"If Steve doesn't return in the next few minutes, I'll look for her, too," Jaxson said.

I hoped that wouldn't be necessary. I would die if anything happened to her.

Aunt Fern came over and hugged me. "How are you doing?"

While everyone meant well in asking, it was getting to be a bit tiresome. "Good." I nodded to her oversized purse. "Did Iggy convince you to let him come."

I'd turned down his request, because I knew he'd be upset.

"He wanted to, but then he and Aimee decided to spend the evening together."

I couldn't imagine what those two had in common. They both wanted to be the most important person in the room. Just then Steve returned, and who should be by his side but Rihanna and apparently her new friend Gavin Sanchez. I wanted to throttle her and hug her at the same time.

As I started to move toward her, Jaxson gently clasped my upper arm. "Let it go, Glinda. Rihanna has been through a lot."

"I need to know if she was trying to chase after that warlock."

"Can you ask her tomorrow? She's safe now."

Jaxson always was one to think straight. "Sure."

My mother came toward me with her sister in tow. I couldn't even remember the last time I'd seen my aunt, but I had to admit she looked better than I remembered.

After I hugged her, I told her how sorry I was about Uncle Lucas.

"Me, too." She clasped my hand. "Thanks for helping Rihanna. She really seems happy here."

"I hope so."

We talked for a bit more, and then my mom suggested her sister lie down. It was a good idea since the service was winding down, and I, too, felt the strain of it.

Aunt Tricia placed a hand on my shoulder. "Call me sometime, okay?"

"I will."

My mom escorted her sister out, probably to the Magic Wand Hotel. I'm sure if my mother had room, she would have put up my aunt.

"Let me walk you home," Jaxson said.

Considering my apartment was only a few feet away, I didn't see the need, but I always enjoyed his company. Jaxson even escorted me to the top of the stairs.

"Are you going to be okay?" he asked.

"I am, but do me a favor?"

"Anything."

"Can you stop at the office and make sure Rihanna gets home okay? If I talk to her, I'm afraid I'll yell at her for scaring me to death."

He smiled. "I'll be happy to."

Jaxson leaned down and kissed me on the cheek. "Sleep well."

A bit stunned by his action, I touched my face. Before I could even respond, Iggy came out of my aunt's apartment. "About time you got home."

Way to go, Iggy. "Thanks, Jaxson. See you tomorrow."

"For sure, and don't worry about Rihanna."

"I'll try."

I opened my apartment door and escorted Iggy inside. He turned around and faced me. "Tell me everything and leave nothing out."

I had to smile. At least some things never changed.

MY CELL BUZZED the next morning, jarring me out of my deep sleep. I wouldn't have minded so much if I hadn't lay in bed wide awake for way too many hours and only recently drifted off to sleep. When I lifted my phone off the dresser, I smiled. It was Jaxson.

"Hey. I'm guessing that Rihanna got in okay last night?" I asked.

"In fact, she was at the office with Gavin when I returned. I think I embarrassed her."

That made me laugh. "I can only imagine. Did you give them some excuse why you were at the office so late?"

"You know me well. I did. I said I needed my computer. I grabbed it and left."

"Did Rihanna say whether she saw the blond-haired man or anything?"

"No," Jaxson said. "And I didn't ask."

Jaxson was better at those kinds of things than I was. "That was probably wise. I'm about to head into the office now."

"I was wondering, since Rihanna is at school, if you wanted to have a bite to eat at the diner first?"

That was unexpected, but Jaxson was well aware I could always eat. "Sure. I can meet you in fifteen minutes."

"I'll snag us a table."

I quickly changed and went into the living room. I never knew where Iggy might be—here or at the office—so I called out to him. "Iggy, you here?"

He popped his head out from the kitchen. "Yes."

"I'm going to the diner. Do you want to come?" I knew the answer, but he liked to be asked.

"What do you think?"

"Smart aleck." I grabbed my purse and placed him inside.

When we made it to the diner, Jaxson waved from the back, and I slipped in across from him. Iggy jumped out of my purse and crawled onto the table.

"Iggy, you can't be up there."

"I'm just crossing over to Jaxson."

He was a traitor. Jax grinned. "Come on, buddy. Sit by me."

A waitress stopped over, and I ordered French Toast and coffee, while Jax did his usual scrambled eggs and coffee thing.

"What's up?" I asked.

"I asked Rihanna to send me the picture of the blond man who was at the service last night."

I liked where this was headed. "And?"

"I thought we could show it to Steve and maybe Gertrude. You said she might have an idea who was able to open locks with their minds."

"She said she'd look into it, but we can certainly show it to her."

"Good."

Dolly emerged from the back and delivered two meals to another table. She then came over to us. "I'm beginning to think you like my diner better than your aunt's restaurant."

Was that true? The food was equally good, but Dolly usually had the time to chat. Plus, she never gave me warnings about something being too dangerous. I smiled. "Maybe."

"How is Rihanna holding up?" Dolly had been to the viewing.

"She seems to be dealing with it quite well. It could be because I think she has a new male friend." Even though the first time they'd spoken was at her father's funeral, they seemed to hit it off.

Dolly's brows rose. "Do I know this young man?"

"Maybe. It's Dr. Sanchez's son who is here to study with her for the year."

"Gavin. Yes. We've met. Quite the eye-catcher."

I laughed. "I suppose." I turned to Jaxson. "Would you mind showing Dolly the photo that Rihanna took?"

His brows didn't actually pinch, but I got the sense he wished I hadn't asked, though I had no idea why. We needed all the help we could get.

He pulled the image up on his phone. "Do you know who this guy is?"

Dolly studied the picture. "Not his name, but he's been in here a time or two."

My pulse shot up. "You wouldn't happen to remember the last time he came in, would you?"

"Sweetie, I remember a lot, but mostly the locals. So, no."

That was disappointing. "If he ever shows up again, can you call me?"

"Why is he so important?"

I glanced over at Jaxson. I wanted him to field the question. "It's a long shot, but he could be a person of interest," Jaxson said.

"Ooh. Then I'll be sure to be extra diligent."

Our meals arrived, and the server placed them in front of us. "Thank you. When is Pearl coming back?" I asked.

"Tomorrow, thank goodness. We have so much to catch up on."

I could only imagine. "I'm sure you do."

We were partially through our meal when the server returned with a plate of lettuce. "Dolly thought you might like this."

"Yes, and tell her thank you."

"At least someone cares about me," Iggy mumbled.

I could only chuckle. Jaxson picked up the plate, and when he placed it on the seat next to him, Iggy went to town.

Just as we finished, my phone rang. "It's Steve." I swiped

the icon. I would have put it on speaker, but I didn't want the whole diner to hear it. "Hello?"

"Glinda, it's Steve. We got lucky."

My pulse soared. I didn't want to speculate that he found the blond man. "How so?"

"Long story, but did you know that Frank Sanchez is an amateur photographer?"

"I had no idea."

"Well, he is, and he has his own darkroom. When his grandson told him about the film camera that Rihanna turned into me, he offered to develop the film."

"That's great. Do you have the photos yet?"

"I do. It's why I'm calling. Stop on by anytime."

"Thanks." I disconnected and told Jaxson about the prints.

"Did he say what they were of?"

"No, but I had the sense it wasn't about any robbery."

We finished up, paid, and then headed across the street. Jennifer was there and waved us back. I knocked on Steve's door.

"Come in."

Once inside, Steve handed us a folder. "I thought you'd want to look these over before handing them to Rihanna."

That didn't sound good. "Why?"

"You said her father never contacted her until he showed up as her photo teacher."

"That's right."

"These pictures were taken over many years. I'm actually surprised the film was still good. They're of her over the years."

My pulse soared. "He was stalking her?"

"I'm not sure I'd call it that. Think about it. If he was this secretive Black Ops guy, I can see why he'd have to be careful. He wanted to get to know his daughter as long as no one else was aware of it."

"I get it. Having your only child believe you're dead couldn't have been easy on him either."

"No."

Together, Jaxson and I looked at the photos. Only in a few of them did Rihanna look truly happy, and that saddened me. I couldn't imagine seeing my child grow and not be able to hold her. "Thanks for these."

"Sure."

"Anything on the other camera?" I asked.

He pulled open his drawer. "Not much. Everything was recent. I'm guessing he deleted his photos from when he was working overseas." Steve handed both cameras back to me, along with the flash drive.

I stuffed one in my purse and slung the larger one over my shoulder. "I appreciate it. You said you were going to contact the school about my uncle's employment to see if they knew anything else about him. Did anything come of it?"

Steve's lips pressed together. "I did, but it was a dead end. The real photo teacher was taking an eight-week maternity leave. Mr. Tillman, or rather Mr. Samuels, was only hired on a temporary basis, which was why they didn't do much of a background check. All I could find out was that some board member recommended him."

Jaxson nodded. "He probably received a call from some military guy vouching for Joe Tillman."

"Probably so. If his operations were that secret, we might never learn who Samuels' boss was. That being said, it appears as if his death didn't have anything to do with his past," Steve said.

"I agree. Finding a very talented thief who can disappear at will might be harder than locating some angry terrorist anyway."

"Sad, but true."

Chapter Eleven

I POINTED TO Jaxson. "Before we go, show the sheriff the picture Rihanna took."

"I guess it can't hurt." He pulled up the shot and pressed a few buttons. "I just emailed it to you."

"Thanks. What is it of?"

"This is the man I told you about. The one Rihanna saw hovering over her dad's coffin."

"Right, and she heard his thoughts about him being happy her dad was dead," Steve said.

"Yes."

"What do you think?" he asked me.

"Honestly, I don't know. Just because he had blond hair doesn't make him a killer. However, Rihanna has often read my thoughts, so maybe the guy did taser both men."

"Glinda, even I can often tell what you're thinking. You don't hide your emotions very well," Steve said.

Now I was insulted. I turned to Jaxson for support. "Is that true?"

"I'm afraid so, pink lady."

"Okay, what am I thinking now?"

Jaxson blew out a breath. "That you will show us that you can block us from your thoughts. While you might succeed for a short while, you can't hide for long."

Jerk.

Steve finished studying the image. "It's clear enough. I can try to do facial recognition on the guy, but if he doesn't have a record, his name won't show up on any database."

"He doesn't look very old either, maybe twenty-three. If he can disappear from view, I bet he hasn't been caught yet."

"You might be right, but I'll send his photo to the neighboring towns. Someone might know him."

"Great."

With our work done here, Jaxson and I left. Because Lucas Samuels was indeed gone, it was time to let the Beachside Condos know what we wanted to do with his place.

At the sales office, we spoke with the manager, Samantha Darling, again. She'd been the one Jaxson had interviewed recently about another murder. I was pleased to see the very attractive woman showed little interest in him. Yes, I had been a little jealous at the time, but who wouldn't be? Jaxson was a great catch.

For some bizarre reason, my uncle had actually purchased the place instead of just renting it. What I couldn't figure out was if his job was only temporary, what did he plan to do afterward? Stay in Witch's Cove and live off of his military retirement?

We'd already conferred with Rihanna about what to do with his place. As much as she'd like to live in such a nice place, she wasn't sure where she'd even be in a year, so she suggested we should sell it.

I thought that was very mature on her part. I had then called my mom to ask her what she thought we should do.

She spoke with Aunt Tricia who agreed with Rihanna.

"Once the property goes through probate, I'll be happy to list it. While it's not totally legal to let you go through his things, I trust you, Glinda. I suggest you clean out any personal effects first. In my experience, selling it furnished will be much easier than if it's left empty."

"Good to know. I'll send the sale documents to my aunt to sign."

The problem was that I didn't know if that was legal. Aunt Tricia and my uncle were divorced, and she was a recovering drug addict. If my uncle had a will, where was it? I didn't have a will yet. I mean, I'm young. I could only hope that my uncle was more forward thinking, especially since he had a child.

Jaxson placed a hand on my back. "Let's go back to the cheese shop and pick up some boxes. We have tons."

"I like that idea. Got any tape?"

"We do."

"We need to wait for Rihanna to get home. She needs to be the one to help pack," I said.

"I bet you're hoping Rihanna might touch something and learn more about her dad."

I guess my thoughts were rather transparent. "Is that a bad thing?"

"No, come on."

We returned to the office and waited for Rihanna to get home from school. When she finally arrived, she looked tired.

"How was your day?" I know I hated being asked that question the moment I stepped foot in the house, but it seemed like the right thing to ask.

"Fine. I'm going to start my homework."

That was her way of avoiding talking about things. "We need to talk."

She faced me. "Is this about Gertrude? Did you book our next appointment?"

I loved her excitement. "Not yet, but I will. There is something we need to do first."

"More shopping?" she asked, though this time she didn't sound all that excited about buying more clothes that weren't black.

"No." I explained about needing to clean out the condo. "We can donate his clothes, but there might be some papers he has that will help us understand what was going on in his life."

"Sure. Whatever."

At least she didn't say no. I turned to Jaxson. "Ready to head out?"

"Definitely."

After picking up the empty boxes, some trash bags, packing tape, and a few markers to make notes as to what was in each box, from Drake's store, Jaxson headed to the Beachside Condos. As we neared, I realized how hard this would be on all of us. I didn't remember much about my uncle, but he was Rihanna's flesh and blood.

She didn't say anything on the way over nor when we entered the condo.

"Where do you want me to start?" she finally asked.

I turned to Jaxson. "How about I tackle the kitchen, and you and Rihanna take his bedroom?"

My logic was that if she had a vision, she might be more

willing to share without me asking her every few minutes if she saw or felt something.

"Sounds good," he said.

What little food there was, I threw out. My uncle clearly was not a cook. I left the few plates, cups, and other dishes that he had in the cabinets for the new owners. During my clean up attempt, I found nothing of value.

I'd already checked the second bedroom. The dresser drawers and closet were empty. I would ask Rihanna if she wanted to keep the photos that were over the bed or the decorative pillows since she seemed to connect with them.

The living room produced nothing either. I had to hope that Jaxson and Rihanna had been more successful. When I stepped into Uncle Lucas' bedroom, three garbage bags that I assumed contained my uncle's clothes were piled up at one end.

"Find anything?" I asked.

"Not yet," Jaxson said. "The guy sure did travel light."

"If he's moved and changed his name as often as I imagine he has, he's learned how to do so."

"Yeah, which is kind of sad. No memories," Jaxson said.

That would be sad.

Jaxson reached up to the top shelf and pulled down some kind of folder. He opened it. "Jackpot. I can't believe I didn't find this before."

Rihanna and I rushed over. "What is it?"

"His papers. As in his real ones. I wouldn't be surprised if he'd kept them in a safety deposit box somewhere all these years."

He handed them to me, and I looked them over. "Wow.

My uncle's driver's license." I sniffled. "He looks so young."

Rihanna moved next to me. "May I see?"

"Of course." I handed it to her.

Next I found his divorce papers and quickly stuffed them in the back. The two-page document after that was what I was hoping to find. "Here is his will." I quickly read it. "Your dad left you and your mom his entire estate. This condo is worth a lot, but I don't know what else he has."

"I doubt much more. It's so sad that he's gone," she said.

"I know."

Rihanna returned to her side of the room. She was hurting, but I didn't know what I could do to help her.

Once we finished, we dropped Rihanna back off at the office since she wanted to start on her homework. Jaxson and I then dumped or donated most of his things. As for his papers, we thought they'd be okay at the office for now.

"Maybe we should get a real safe," he said.

"I agree. One with an eye scanner."

He knew why I suggested that. "I'll look into it."

When we were finished, I decided to go home. I wouldn't be fit company for sharing dinner with either Jaxson or Rihanna.

Once back in my apartment, I made an appointment with Gertrude for tomorrow after Rihanna came home from school. With my chores done, I headed into the bathroom for a long soak in the tub.

"DID GERTRUDE SAY what we're doing today?" my cousin

asked.

"No, but I'm sure it will be good."

We checked in at the Psychics Corner reception desk and then went to Gertrude's office. Whoa. "Mom? What's going on?"

She spun to face me. "We thought it was time to see whether Rihanna can contact someone who's passed over."

"I've never spoken to anyone who has died," she said.

I touched her arm. "That's not true. You heard what your dad said when you touched his clothes."

She seemed to need time to think about it. "I guess, but that was by chance."

"Would you like to try to talk to someone else today?" Gertrude asked.

"Someone else? Why not my dad?"

Gertrude motioned we take a seat at the large round table she'd set up. "I don't believe he's ready. I imagine your father needs to take care of some business first."

"What do you mean?" Rihanna asked.

"Not that I've spoken to every person who has died, but in the case of those souls whose lives have been taken from them, they often need to see justice served first before they are ready to rest. Considering how powerful your dad was, I imagine he will find the right time and place to talk to you. He might not be ready yet."

Rihanna's chin wobbled. "Okay."

I always thought that the souls only talked before they crossed over, but what did I know? "If not Uncle Lucas, then who?"

My mother clasped my hand. "I thought we could talk to

my mother."

I instantly touched my necklace that had been a present from her. "Nana? Really?"

"I haven't tried in years, but if the four of us put our powers together, I'm willing to bet she'd want to talk to her two granddaughters."

I looked at Rihanna. "Are you okay with this?"

"Sure."

Once we were seated, Gertrude lit the four candles on the table and then dimmed the lights in the room via some remote-control device. Go Gertrude. She then placed the palms of her hands on the table, face down. "Please do the same, making sure that your fingertips touch the person's next to you."

Even though I'd seen this done before, I'd never partici-pated in an actual séance. Sure, I'd been with my mom when she spoke to someone who'd died, but that was always a one-way conversation. The only exception was when the person she contacted spoke to me instead. A slight shiver shot through me at that thought.

"Close your eyes," Gertrude said. "Picture Amelia, if you can."

Knowing the relationship between Aunt Tricia and her mom hadn't been the best, I wasn't sure if Rihanna had even seen a picture of our grandmother. Seeing her in her mind's eye then could be difficult.

I expected more instructions, but none came. Instead, Gertrude called out to my grandmother to join us however she wished to appear. I thought that a bit odd, but who was I to question the great Gertrude Poole?

With my eyes still shut, and my fingers touching my mother's and Rihanna's, I jerked when a cold breeze swept across my face. I couldn't help but open my eyes.

But what I saw wasn't at all what I expected. "Nana?"

Chapter Twelve

STANDING BEHIND GERTRUDE was the apparition of my grandmother. I blinked a few times to make sure I wasn't imagining her. Because I believed she'd crossed over a long time ago, never in a million years did I expect to see her ghostly form. I might have thought it was some parlor trick, but it was clearly my grandmother. I wanted to lift my hands to touch my necklace, but I feared it might break the connection.

"Ah….guys?"

The others opened their eyes. I held my breath waiting to see if they could see her too.

"Mom?" my mother said, her voice wavering.

My breath whooshed out. I wasn't crazy after all.

"Yes, it's me. I need to thank Gertrude for calling me." Nana's voice sounded strong, for which I was pleased. Because she was rather transparent, I couldn't quite tell her level of health—not that ghosts even had a health level.

I wanted to jump up, run to her, and hug my grandmother, but I'd had enough experience with ghosts to know that wasn't how it worked.

"I miss you," I blurted, wanting her to know there wasn't a day that went by without me thinking of her.

"Glinda. I miss you more than you can imagine. You have done so well, and may I say I'm happy you are embracing your powers." She turned to Rihanna and opened her arms. "And you, my little darling, Rihanna. Oh, how I wished I'd been there for you growing up."

My cousin's mouth opened, but nothing came out. I couldn't blame her. This probably was the first time Rihanna had seen a ghost. She was so lucky to see one without having to drink some pink potion first. Maybe it was that my cousin was just that talented.

My grandmother's image faded for a moment, or was it my watery eyes that were making it hard to see? I cleared my throat. "Have you seen Uncle Lucas yet?"

I honestly didn't know how the afterlife worked.

"He's not ready to join me, but I will welcome him when he does. He was a brave and good man. His powers were passed down to Rihanna. Glinda, help her embrace them."

My cousin cleared her throat. "Did a warlock kill him?"

"Yes, my sweet. A very dark one. He must be stopped."

And then she disappeared. I sat there stunned. The candles extinguished, which I thought had to be some kind of trick, but when I looked up at Gertrude, she seemed surprised, too.

Even this late in the day in September, enough light poured into the room for me to see clearly. Gertrude pressed the clicker, and the overhead lights came on.

She inhaled deeply. "I don't think I've ever had a ghost appear at a séance. I did summon her, but I truly thought she'd speak through one of us."

I'd never seen Gertrude flustered. "I, for one, am thrilled

to have seen her again." My grandmother meant the world to me.

"I think it was your abilities, Glinda, that helped her come through," Gertrude said.

"Mine?" I considered my witch abilities to be the least powerful in the group.

"Yes. Yours. You have spoken with ghosts recently." She pushed back her chair. "And if what Amelia said was true about the dark warlock, then I have work to do too."

I looked over at Rihanna. "Would you show Gertrude the picture of the man at the memorial service? She might recognize him."

"Sure." She pulled out her phone and showed Gertrude the blond man who'd been leaning over her father's coffin.

"Oh, my."

My pulse pounded in the vein at my temple. "You know him?"

"I just might. I have some calls to make."

The three of us pushed back our chairs. After Rihanna sent the picture to Gertrude, we thanked her and left. This time, my mom insisted on paying for the session. She held out her hand. "I'm still shaking. Gertrude told me she'd try to contact my mother, but I only expected to hear her voice."

"I know, right?"

"My whole body is vibrating," Rihanna said. "A ghost? Really? I didn't know my grandmother, but what just happened was nothing like I've ever experienced before."

"Seeing her ghost appear like that was a bit disconcerting. I know Amelia implied your dad wasn't ready to communicate, but I wish you could have contacted him."

"Me, too," Rihanna said. "Even if it was just to tell him that I love him, despite him being absent when I was growing up."

"That's a nice thing to say."

We walked back to the office, where my mother hugged us goodbye. Having Rihanna here seemed to have brought out her emotional side, and I liked it.

I thought it might be time to show Rihanna the pictures her father had taken of her. I hoped it wouldn't change her opinion of him.

Inside, Jaxson was there. "How did it go?" he asked.

I held up my hands. "You won't believe it."

"I'll get you ladies some iced tea. You look like you could use some."

Part of me wanted to hug him, but something inside told me to hold off a little longer.

When Jaxson placed the drinks on the coffee table, I pulled out the pictures her dad had taken. "These photos came from your father's Hasselblad. The sheriff found someone to develop them." I handed them to her.

Rihanna studied them carefully. It seemed as if it took her a minute to realize some of the first ones were of her. She looked up at me. "My dad took pictures of *me*?"

"Apparently, but he didn't tell you, because he couldn't let anyone know you were his daughter."

She nodded. "I know. That would have put me and my mom in danger."

I had to admit, Rihanna was taking it very well. As she looked at the rest of the pictures, tears streamed down her cheeks. "This is me coming down the stairs of this office. He knew where I lived. Why didn't he tell me sooner?"

"You said it yourself," I reminded her. "He wanted to talk to you on Monday. I'm betting he would have told you everything then."

"Why did he have to die?"

There it was. The question we all wanted to know. "I doubt it was his choice."

"Yes, it was. He didn't have to try to be some hero and go after those guys."

I had wondered that, too. "While I can't know what was in his head, I'm betting your father could sense what kind of person the blond man was. If he believed the man to be evil, he would want to put a stop to it. It was the type of man that he was."

"I guess. Do you think Gertrude will pull through in locating the blond man?"

"I'm hoping."

"Ladies," Jaxson said. "Tell me about your session. It sounds quite remarkable."

"That was an understatement."

Even after we explained that my grandmother appeared to us, it was hard to believe it had actually happened. If the others hadn't seen her, I might have thought I'd lost my mind. Because I couldn't sense Iggy's ghost cat, I figured I no longer possessed the ability to see apparitions. I now know I'd been wrong.

THE NEXT DAY, I did some legwork for the case, but I ended

my search around three since I wanted to be back at the office when Rihanna returned home from school. I was hurrying up the steps to the office when my cell rang. I yanked open the door and stepped inside to answer it.

Jaxson looked over and smiled. The caller ID showed it was Gertrude. We didn't have an appointment today, so I was surprised she was contacting me.

"Hey, Gertrude."

"Glinda, I may have a lead on the boys who are stealing things and who also killed the two innocent bystanders."

I don't know how Jaxson did it, but he was by my side in a flash. My face must have paled or something. My knees had definitely wobbled. He led me over to the sofa and guided me to sit down. He nodded to the phone.

"I'm going to put you on speaker so Jaxson can hear." I pressed the button. "Okay, go ahead."

"I reached out to my grandson, Levy Poole. He runs a coven over in Hampton River of very powerful witches and warlocks."

That was a few towns away. "Did he recognize the blond man?"

"He did. He goes by the name of Steward Winthrop."

"What does *goes by the name of* mean?"

"He changes it often, which means he won't be in the sheriff's system."

Darn. "Does your grandson have any way of finding out if this man is behind the murders?"

"Not really, but he will put his feelers out. He thinks someone in the community will know his whereabouts. But Glinda, even if you found out where he lives, and you knock on his door—"

I didn't need her to finish the sentence. "I know. We have no proof that he did anything wrong."

"That's right, but that doesn't mean it's hopeless. There is something we can do."

"What's that?"

The door to our office opened, and Rihanna came in. I motioned her over and mouthed it was Gertrude. Interest sparked in her eyes as she sat across from us.

"I told my grandson about Rihanna's talents. He would like to train her. He thinks she may be the key to solving this."

I sucked in a breath. Involve Rihanna? I wasn't so sure about that. Besides, I didn't know her grandson. If he hadn't been related to Gertrude, I would have said no instantly. Before I did, I wanted to find out more. "What can he help her with?"

"Not only can he read minds, though maybe not as well as Rihanna's father could, my grandson can open locks with his mind."

That was not what I expected her to say. No wonder she'd reacted rather strangely when I mentioned how the thief had entered the house. "Am I to assume he can cloak himself, too?"

"He can, and so can others that he knows. Like I said, he is with a very powerful coven. Some of the members have abused their power. That is why Levy is questioning whether he even wants to stay with them."

Decisions, decisions. "Let me talk it over with Rihanna and Jaxson. We'll let you know."

"Of course. I believe you mentioned that the robberies

were taking place every five days, right?"

"Yes."

"Then the clock is ticking."

"I know," I said. "And thank you."

I disconnected. My head wasn't able to grasp all of this.

"I want to do it," Rihanna said.

"I don't know anything about this Levy guy."

"Glinda," Jaxson said. "You trust Gertrude, and this is her grandson. She wouldn't suggest Rihanna train with him unless he was trustworthy."

I knew it was for the best, and it might be the only way to catch this killer, but she was only a teenager. "I know. I'll talk to Mom and see what she says."

Before I could lift my phone to call her, it was as if someone pressed ice cubes to my cheeks. I stilled at the unexpected cold. Iggy jumped up on my lap. "Who's that?" my familiar asked.

I looked around but didn't see anyone. "Where?"

"Right in front of you," my iguana said.

"Are you talking about my grandmother?" Iggy knew her quite well, and he could see ghosts.

"Yes."

"Glinda, your necklace is glowing," Jaxson said.

What the heck? I looked down, and the moment I clasped it, my grandmother's image appeared to me. "Nana?"

"Yes, my sweet. I don't have much time, but please let Rihanna train under Levy. He'll be good for her. It's up to you two to catch these men. None of the sheriffs have the ability."

And then she was gone.

Me? I was the first to believe Rihanna had a lot of talent, but my spells went awry more than they worked.

"What just happened?" Jaxson asked.

"My grandmother came back." I told him what she'd said. I turned to Rihanna. "You saw her, right?"

"Not this time. Only at Gertrude's."

Okay, this witch stuff was getting out of control.

Chapter Thirteen

"DRINK SOME TEA." Jaxson held up my glass.

I took a sip. "Thanks."

"What did Grandma say exactly?" Rihanna asked.

I told them about her desire to have Rihanna train under Levy.

Jaxson scooted closer. "She might be right. If Gertrude's grandson knows this thief and says the man can open locks with his mind, do you really think Steve, or the sheriff of Hampton River, can stop him?"

That was the problem. "No, but I'd still like to talk to my mom about it. First though, I want to tell Steve what I learned. Would you mind staying here with Rihanna?"

"I'm not going to run away," Rihanna interjected.

"I know, but I'd feel better if Jax is here, in case you want to talk to someone about what happened." I nodded to the photos.

"Sure."

Before she changed her mind, I headed over to the sheriff's office. To my delight, Pearl was back.

I grinned. "How was your hiatus?"

She waved a hand. "It's nice to visit with the rest of my family, but I always miss Witch's Cove."

In other words, she missed being in the loop. "I get it. Is Steve in?"

"He sure is."

I always expected him to be off investigating, but once more, I got lucky. Heading back to his office, I noticed Nash's desk was empty, implying Steve had him doing the legwork. I knocked on the sheriff's door and entered.

"Glinda, I'm beginning to think you've started working here, and no one told me."

He was kidding, but it seemed that way to me, too. "I know the name of the man who I believe committed all of the thefts."

Without prompting, I pulled up a chair, while Steve located his yellow note pad. If he ever lost that thing, he'd be in a world of hurt. On the other hand, if anyone hacked his computer, they wouldn't find his notes.

"Tell me," he said.

"The blond man currently goes by the name of Steward Winthrop, but that is an alias. Apparently, he changes it often. He's from Hampton River."

"And how did you find this out?"

I decided to skip the séance and ghost sighting and go straight to Gertrude's phone call.

"And this Levy Poole is her grandson?"

"Yes, and she trusts him implicitly."

"Why, don't you?"

"I've yet to see his talents in action, but he claims that he, too, can open locks with his mind. And he can cloak himself."

Steve jotted down the information. "This is not anything I can use to bring in Mr. Winthrop for questioning though."

"No, but I'm thinking the sheriff in Hampton River might be aware of the man's comings and goings."

"I'll let him know. Anything else?"

"Let's say for the sake of argument that this man did kill my uncle as well as the other homeowner, how do you think an ordinary human can catch him?"

Steve's eyes slightly narrowed. Being called an ordinary human didn't seem to sit well with him. "I don't know. Do you have a plan?"

"Not yet, but I'm working on it." I held up my hand since I knew how his mind worked. He wanted to tell me to stay out of it. "Don't worry. Anything I do will strictly be from a distance. I'll let you and the sheriff from Hampton River do the heavy lifting, but you will need help."

"You are probably right." He opened his desk drawer. "I received the autopsy report back from Dr. Sanchez who compared the taser marks from your uncle to this homeowner's. She concluded they were from the same taser. The strength was boosted to an extremely high, which was what caused each to suffer heart failure."

"Which implied they wanted to kill the person."

"That is what it appears."

That didn't surprise me all that much. "Are you still thinking there might be two people involved?"

"Dr. Sanchez says the angle of the taser was applied at a ninety-degree angle to the back. It would be hard for someone to get behind the homeowner and taser him like that."

I lifted a finger. "Unless he cloaked himself. The homeowner wouldn't know to turn around if he couldn't see him."

"Excellent point. I would agree except that I've watched

the video your uncle took many times. The door to the last home that was robbed opened. Then we see the bike flicker. A second later, your uncle is tasered. I don't see the same person being in two places at once."

I replayed that video in my mind. "You're right. There could have been one man on the inside and a second on the outside as a lookout of sorts. He was the clean-up man should anything go wrong."

"That's a strong possibility."

I figured I should tell him at least the start of my plan. I didn't have all of it worked out in my mind, but I had something. "For starters, Gertrude's grandson is going to train Rihanna."

Yes, I know, I hadn't passed it by my mom, but I believed she'd say yes, especially since Nana was in favor of it.

His mouth pinched, acting as if I told him the man wanted to teach her how to kill. "Train her to do what? Pick locks?"

"No, but that thought had crossed my mind. To improve her ability to read minds. It was what her father excelled at."

"How will that help us?"

"I have an idea about that. Ask the sheriff in Hampton River to follow this guy. If he can let us know when and where the thief goes out to eat, Rihanna and I can head on out there. All she needs to do is be within maybe ten feet or so of this thief to be able to read his mind, assuming she can learn to channel her abilities. If the man doesn't block her, she might be able to hear where his next robbery will take place."

"Does she have super hearing, too?"

"No. Though that gives me an idea. What if she and I go

to this food place and try to get a read on the guy while Nash comes in, too? He's the one with super hearing."

The lines on Steve's face softened. "That just might work. Have you figured out what happens when this man actually robs some place? He'll disappear and leave. Correct me if I'm wrong, but how do you catch a ghost?"

He was mixing up his paranormal beings. "When I was able to cloak myself, I was still there. If you threw a bag of flour on me, you'd see me."

He chuckled. "I can see it now. I'll request a helicopter from the Florida governor, and then ask them to dump a hundred pounds of flour on some poor man's house, hoping a few cups land on the thief so we can see him."

I had to smile at that image. "I think the sound of the helicopter would be enough to make Winthrop change his mind."

"I agree."

I had another thought. "Nash's senses are highly developed. What if we scent the items the man plans to steal? You could put a heap of counterfeit money in the safe that has a distinctive smell that Nash has memorized. Follow the scent, follow the man."

"I do love your imagination, Glinda. The plan certainly has potential. When Nash returns, I will discuss it with him. In the meantime, I need to call the sheriff in Hampton River. If we can't get eyes on this guy, the plan falls apart."

"I agree."

After I chatted with Pearl on the way out, I went to the mortuary. Having discussed part of my plan with Steve, I was feeling a little bit better. I was pretty sure that my mother wouldn't have an issue with Levy Poole training Rihanna.

"WHAT DID AUNT Wendy say?" Rihanna asked when I returned to the office.

"She was in favor of it. It is your heritage, after all. To be honest, I think she wants you to help me improve. We all know my witch's skills aren't reliable."

"That's not true," Rihanna said. "You were able to see Grandma, and I wasn't."

"The fact Iggy could see her might have meant there was some residual effect from when I drank the potion that was supposed to change Iggy from pink to green."

"Maybe."

I waved a hand. "It doesn't matter. Right now, we need you to learn what you can from Levy. I told Steve about the blond man, and who Levy said he was."

"Steve believed you?" Jaxson asked.

"He did. I even outlined a very loose plan on how we can go about nabbing this guy. And by *we*, I mean Rihanna and I will be with Nash Solano when Steward Winthrop is eating at some restaurant. Rihanna can listen into the man's thoughts, while Nash will be there to pick up on any conversation."

"You think you might learn the location of his next heist?" Jaxson asked.

"That's my hope." I explained about Steve notifying the sheriff in Hampton River. "We need to have eyes on this Winthrop guy."

Rihanna leaned forward. "I'm confused about the role of

Nash."

Oh, boy. Now wasn't the time to tell her about him being a werewolf who thankfully could control his shift. "He's the deputy who was born with amazing hearing and sight. I thought it could come in handy."

She smiled. "I like it. All I have to do is sit near Winthrop and try to read his mind as to whose house he might rob next?"

"Yup. That's all."

"Then I guess we need to contact Gertrude and tell her I'm game."

I appreciated my cousin's spunk. "I will, but I'm going to ask that Levy meet you here."

Her brows pinched. "You don't trust him?"

"That's not it. I think it's safer if no one connects the two of you. If anyone sees Levy entering our office, they'll think he's here to hire us."

"Works for me."

I called Gertrude back and set up a time for tomorrow after Rihanna returned from school. I realized that he might not be able to teach her everything at once, but it was a start. We really didn't have a lot of time.

I disconnected. "We're all set. Gertrude mentioned that for this to work, we needed to be as unobtrusive as possible. She said the two of us always stand out."

"Don't tell me she wants me to wear some tacky slogan T-shirt, blue jeans, and pink lipstick?" Rihanna said.

She acted as if that would be the worst thing in the world. My duty was to help her. "If you do that, I'll do you one better."

Rihanna smiled. "Oh, this I've got to see."

"Glinda?" Jaxson said. "What are you planning?"

"Nothing permanent, but I might put a brown rinse on my hair."

He sucked in a breath, pretending to be horrified. Then a smile captured his face. "You are a good sport."

I wagged a finger at him. "It's only temporary."

"Sure."

Since the shops would only be open for another couple of hours, I stood. "We don't have time to dawdle," I told my cousin.

"For the record, this goes against everything I stand for, but if we have any hope of catching the man who killed my father, I have to do this."

"I agree."

I thought it would be easy—or kind of easy—until I actually entered the store. My plan was to grab some new clothes and then get our hair done. Priscilla's spa was open until eight. If Rihanna was feeling daring, she might even change her nail polish.

"I don't know where to begin." My cousin was browsing through a stack of jeans.

"You just need to look like every other high school teenager."

"Gross."

I chuckled. "I'm going to struggle, too. I hate trying on jeans, even if they are pink. Maybe if I go with a dark blue, it will make me look slimmer." Being short had its drawbacks.

"I'll get some blue jeans, too. If the two of us match though, it would be a dead giveaway that we are undercover.

How about we go our separate ways and meet up in about thirty minutes?"

"Sounds good. Just text me when you're done." I was sure that was all the time I'd need.

Finding jeans that fit though took forever, but I eventually grabbed something that didn't make me look like a teapot. I picked out a pretty powder blue top that was actually flattering. Wearing my usual pink Converse sneakers would look strange, so I snatched up a pair of white sneakers. I looked so ordinary I wanted to scream, but I told myself we had to look boring.

I checked out and waited for Rihanna who finished two minutes later. I was actually excited to see what she picked. "Ready to do something with our hair?" I asked.

"Maybe."

"Don't worry. You can dye it black afterward," I said.

"How do you know I dye my hair?"

"Neither of your parents have hair that dark."

A small smile filled her face. "Good detective work."

"Ready for the final step?" I asked.

"You bet."

Chapter Fourteen

I T WAS STUPID that I was nervous to show Jaxson my new look. He wouldn't laugh, but for some reason, I wanted his approval. Why? Because he was becoming more important to me than just someone who could help make my business a success. He'd become my equal partner in The Pink Iguana Sleuth Agency.

If I were to be totally truthful, he'd become more than that. We clicked, and I don't ever remember feeling this comfortable with a guy before, except for maybe Drake. Perhaps it was in the Harrison genes to make me feel safe and liked.

When Rihanna and I had returned from getting our hair done, Jaxson wasn't there. Even Iggy had abandoned ship. After telling Rihanna how proud I was of her for going with some light brown highlights, I headed home. She was fine with that since she claimed she had a lot of homework to do.

When I returned to the office the next day, I decided to wear my usual pink clothes. I'd wait to show them off on the day we had to spy on Mr. Winthrop.

Jaxson was at his usual spot at his desk. He looked up. "I like the brown, but I'm used to you being blonde."

"Me, too. Don't worry. Putting a dark rinse on my hair

myself is too much trouble and going to the salon is too expensive. I'll be sticking to my natural color, thank you." I nodded to the computer. "Any news about Hampton River?"

"Steve hasn't called if that's what you're asking, nor have I found out anything useful. I have to agree with Levy that Steward Winthrop is not the guy's real name."

I dropped down on the sofa. "Darn. It doesn't really matter. What we need to figure out is what we're going to do once we know where this secretive man's next target will be."

Jaxson pushed back his chair. "Tell me about being invisible."

I hadn't expected that question, but it was a logical one, though Jaxson had been with me almost every time I had cloaked myself. "As you are aware, invisible doesn't mean I'm not there, but it does mean anything I'm holding can't be seen either."

"Which was how you were able to use your camera phone in the dark woods while you were cloaked, and no one could see it glow."

"Exactly."

"That's unfortunate, because it means all of his loot will be invisible, too," Jaxson said.

"I'm afraid so."

Jaxson leaned back in his chair. "What caused you to lose your invisibility shield?"

"Since I've only done it a few times, it's hard to be certain if my experience is anything like that of a pro."

"Try me," he said.

"For me, the moment I lost my focus, I reappeared."

Jaxson sat there for a moment. "If say, Steve shot a gun in

the air, it might startle Winthrop into appearing."

"Sure, but if he is as talented as I think he is, he'll cloak himself right away."

Jaxson nodded. "That confirms what the neighbor saw. Winthrop—assuming he was the thief—flickered. Uncloaked one second and recloaked the next."

"Yes."

Jaxson picked up a pen from his desk and twirled it rather deftly over his knuckles. "Did Levy say how many people in his clan could open locks with their minds?"

"I never thought to ask, but I hope not many. We'll have to check it out when Levy comes by."

"We'll need to, because what if Winthrop only breaks into a house every third time, and his fellow clan members rob a house the other times? He could have an alibi for some of the thefts, which would make it hard to prove he was guilty of any murder."

I sank back against the sofa. "We might never find out who killed Rihanna's dad."

Jaxson nodded. "We need to be mentally prepared for that."

"That is depressing. Suppose Rihanna reads Winthrop's mind and learns when and where his next heist is? Even if we manage to capture him, there is no guarantee he committed the other thefts or murdered anyone."

"True."

My mind spun. "If he is in a coven, I wouldn't be surprised if after we capture him, there is a rash of similar thefts just to cast doubt on Winthrop's guilt. In the end, he might go down for burglary but not for murder."

"Glinda, don't do this to yourself. Let's focus on trying to catch one thief at a time. We'll worry about the murder charge later."

Easy for him to say, though Jaxson was right. I had a tendency to obsess over things. "I imagine Steve will ask the sheriff over at Hampton River to look into Winthrop's whereabouts on the days of the other robberies."

"Let's hope," he said.

"Rihanna said something to me that might be useful." I wasn't sure if I could pull it off, but I had to at least ask.

"What's that?"

"I don't even know if it can be done—by anyone—but what if I could create some kind of shield around the targeted house that would prevent anyone from getting through?"

He huffed out a laugh. "I think you've watched too many sci-fi movies. I doubt force fields exist."

"For ordinary humans maybe."

Jaxson smiled and then held up his hands. "I say give it a try. I never thought anyone could become invisible, and yet you pulled it off. I was going to put my money on Nash being able to follow the scent of the money in the safe and maybe throwing a sheet over the guy, but a shield around the house might prove more useful."

"We might need both. If Nash lets go of him, even for a second, the thief could toss off the sheet and run. There has to be a way to contain him afterward."

Jaxson stood. "I need a soda. Want me to pour you a tea?"

"I'd love one."

Iggy pranced over and climbed up on the sofa. "Why don't you ask me for my advice?"

I had been ignoring him of late. "I'm sorry. You're right. I would love your input."

"Okay. Here's what I've been planning."

"I'm listening." I worked hard not to laugh.

"The moment Nash throws the sheet over this guy, the sheriff or someone else could either Taser him or wrap rope around his waist. That way he couldn't get away."

For such a small animal, he had a good mind. "That idea certainly has potential."

Iggy stuck out his chest. "I thought so, too."

Jaxson handed me a glass of iced tea. "Thanks."

He sat next to me. "If you are going ahead with creating some kind of shield, I don't like you being anywhere near the crime scene. Maybe you can put some kind of repellant spell around yourself while you recite the words."

I had to laugh at that. "Like mosquito repellant?"

"Whatever. You need something to keep him from nabbing you. We don't need a ransom demand."

"On me?" I asked.

"Yes, a witch of your caliber would go for a high price."

I loved his protectiveness. "Would you pay to get me back?"

He scrunched up his nose. "I'd be willing to go as high as one hundred dollars."

I whistled. "A whole one hundred. Hmm. I might have to rethink my plan."

Jaxson grinned. "Whatever they ask, I'd find a way to free you."

Jaxson cared for me, and I certainly appreciated it. "Thank you, but I'll keep working on my plan, along with a ton of contingencies. The shield, if it works, will make it so that he can't get near me, even if it only lasts for two to three minutes." I finished sipping my tea. "I'm going to see if Bertha has any suggestions."

"Sounds good, but be back before Rihanna gets home."

"I will." I was actually tempted to lean over and kiss his cheek since Jaxson was such a dear, but I was an emotional coward. "Maybe see what you can dig up on other thefts in the last year in Hampton River."

Jaxson saluted. "Yes, boss."

While he smiled, I had the sense our relationship would be better if I kept my mouth shut. Like that would ever happen.

I would have taken Iggy with me to Hex and Bones Apothecary, but from past experience, he could get lost for hours in that store, and finding him always took time. Besides, I didn't need him scaring any customers.

For once, the store was empty, and I made a beeline to Bertha, who was arranging some candles on a shelf.

"Glinda, always nice to see you. You seem a bit stressed."

I swear the woman was some kind of mind reader. "I am, but before I give you the details, can you tell me if there is a spell that can be put around, say a house, to prevent an occupant from leaving?

She studied me. "Can you be a bit more specific?"

I explained about a thief who could open locks with his mind. "I'm thinking it should be something like a force field. Touch it, and it knocks you back."

She sucked in a breath. "So, this mind bender exists. That is scary stuff."

"I know. He can also cloak himself."

Bertha sighed. "I get it. You can't stop what you can't see."

Because no one was in the store, and I trusted Bertha, I explained my plan in detail. "What do you think?"

"It's quite ingenious. I have something in mind, but this shield would be more like hitting a plexiglass wall rather than actually propelling a person backward."

"That sounds perfect!" If the man was fleeing, hitting anything might toss him on his butt.

"Mind you, it would take practice. A lot of it. How much time do you have?"

"That's the problem. It could be any day now."

Bertha stroked her chin. "I might have something a little bit different, but it, too, would take intense concentration. One wrong word and the whole thing might not work."

Way to be a salesperson. "What do I have to lose? I'm just hoping I won't need it."

"Okay, then. Let me find the spell. Be right back."

As soon as Bertha disappeared, my doubts surfaced. What was I thinking? That I could create some big-time force field that would prevent anyone from leaving an area? And a whole house at that? I couldn't even turn Iggy back to green. Even if I could create this shield, how would I know when to start the spell? We'd have to have some kind of communication device between me, the sheriff, and Nash. That would almost imply that Steve would need to be inside the house in order to signal me when the guy had opened the safe.

A few moments later, Bertha returned with a piece of paper. "I know this seems unorthodox, but this is it. There are no potions to cook, candles to light, or mixture to be made. On the paper you will find the spell you need to recite while you do a series of arm movements."

"That's all? I don't have to run around the house or put stakes at every corner of the property?"

"You will do that using your mind."

Yeah, right. I wanted to give up—but I wouldn't. Too much was at stake—no pun intended. Not only did someone kill my uncle, they murdered another innocent person. Not to mention, they stole money and some very precious items. I wanted assurance it had worked at least once. "Have you ever done this spell?"

"No, I have not, nor do I know of anyone who has."

Great. "How much is it?"

Bertha waved a hand. "If this works, come back, and we'll figure out a fair price."

Oh, boy. Clearly, she anticipated I'd fail. "Thank you for finding this for me."

As I was about to leave, Bertha clasped my wrist. "Dejection and doubt will make you fail." She tapped her temple. "It's all up here. You've got this."

I smiled, but my lips wobbled in the process. "I hope so."

As I left, I wondered if perhaps Levy could give me a few pointers regarding how to focus on the task at hand. Anyone who could unlock doors with his mind should know how to create a shield. I wanted to be able to erect it seconds before the thief ran out of the house with the goods. Sure, it would be great if Nash could pinpoint his location immediately, but I kind of doubted that would happen. I needed Winthrop to run into the shield and lose his concentration long enough for

Nash to nab him. Farfetched? Maybe.

Then there was the issue of whether this theft would occur in the afternoon or at night. At this point, I wasn't sure which I preferred. I probably should have asked Bertha if I needed to be facing in the direction I wanted the shield to be erected. I did believe that if Winthrop spotted me hanging out, say on the sidewalk, he probably wouldn't think anything of it. He'd be arrogant enough to think his ability to remain invisible would prevent anyone from catching him.

I inhaled, hoping I could do this. Wanting to be back at the office before Rihanna showed up, I hurried. I ran up the stairs and entered.

Jaxson turned around. "How did it go?"

I wanted to say great, but I didn't want to lie. "I'm not sure."

"Was there a spell?"

"Yes, but it's something I have to read and kind of act out."

"Act out?"

"Yes. I have to wave my arms in some kind of intricate pattern while I mentally describe where the shield needs to be."

"Oh, is that all?"

Great. Even he could see that it was next to impossible. "I know, right?"

Before I had a chance to study the spell, Rihanna came home. "Is Levy here yet?"

"No."

"Good. I need a drink. I'm so nervous."

"You?" She could already read minds. Levy was there to

help polish her skills. "Why?"

"What if I mess up?" she asked.

"Don't be like me and always doubt yourself. You're not the one who's goofed before."

Of course, leave it to Iggy to rush between us. "Glinda's right. Just look at me. I used to be green."

That again? "Iggy. I was twelve."

"And again, when you were twenty-six," he shot back.

"Yes, I failed to turn you green a few months back, but there were extenuating circumstances."

Thankfully, I was saved from going through defending myself once more, because someone knocked on the office door. "Rihanna, I believe that would be for you."

She flapped her hands, probably to release some energy, and then rushed to answer it. I turned around, curious what someone so powerful would look like.

Rihanna pulled open the door. The man, who was in his early forties just stood there, which I thought rather odd. Perhaps even stranger was that Rihanna seemed to be under his spell and remained almost frozen. Maybe this had been a mistake.

Chapter Fifteen

"RIHANNA, WHY DON'T you ask Levy to come in?" I assumed that was who he was.

"Sorry." Rihanna stepped to the side. "Please."

The rather handsome man entered. "I apologize for just standing there. I've heard so much about Rihanna that I wanted to see for myself whether we were mentally compatible."

What did that mean? "Were you reading her mind?"

He smiled. "I'm betting it was more the other way around."

That was good to hear. "I thought the two of you might want some privacy, so why—"

Jaxson stepped next to me before I could finish my sentence. "So, we'll get out of your hair. We'll go downstairs."

That was a great idea. I was a little leery of any male in Rihanna's bedroom anyway. I turned to Iggy. "Do you want to come with us?"

"Are you kidding? I'm staying here. I want to learn, too."

I don't think that was how it worked, but if he could pick up a few pointers, that would be great. "Okay then."

Jaxson and I took the interior staircase to the cheese and wine store below. "I can't believe how nervous I am for

Rihanna. I want this to go well for her," I said.

"She'll do great."

"I hope so."

Once we were downstairs, he motioned that I follow him into the office. "Tell me about this spell."

That would take my mind off what was happening upstairs. I pulled out the paper and read the spell out loud to him. "Then it gives me a complicated set of arm movements to do while reciting the spell. It seems…"

"Unreliable?"

"More like stupid."

His brows rose. "I thought you believed in magic."

"I do, but I'm not sure I can pull this off."

"Why not? You were able to cloak yourself. How many witches can do that?"

He had a point. So what if disappearing had been so intense that I passed out because of it? "True."

"Why don't we practice right now? We could get a call any moment from Steve telling us where to find this Winthrop guy."

My nerves suddenly flared at that thought. We weren't ready. Any of us. "I can only hope this guy didn't dye his blond curly hair between the time he came to the funeral and the next heist. I might not recognize him."

"I'm sure Rihanna will be able to pick him out."

"Admittedly, she has a photographer's eye for detail."

"How about I read out the arm instructions, and you try to do them? They need to be ingrained in your muscle memory, because I'm betting there will only be seconds between the time the front door of the house opens, and this man takes off, possibly for his bike."

When he stated it like that, it made me more unsure of myself—but I refused to give up. "I'll try."

"Okay. It says here to face the direction of the shield, which should be the house."

"That part is easy. Then what?"

"Swing your right arm in a circle clockwise while your left pans from left to right, parallel to the ground."

I just stood there. Already, it seemed impossible. "I never mastered patting my head and rubbing my stomach at the same time."

Jaxson laughed. "For real?"

I gave him a very sassy look. "Yes, for real. Turn around. I don't want you to watch."

"Why not? I know how hard this is for you."

Why did he have to be so sweet? "Fine. I'll do one arm, then the second arm, and then put them together."

He smiled. "I love when your logical mind takes over."

I inhaled and performed each act separately. Once I succeeded, I tried them at the same time. After doing it fairly well three or four times in a row, I moved on to the second of seven instructions. Jaxson read them to me, and I executed them. Each time, I'd start from the beginning.

After ten minutes of arm pumping and swirling, I was tired. "I need a break."

Jaxson stepped forward and opened his arms. The comfort that action exuded was too much to deny. We both moved into each other's embrace. I pressed my head against his chest and inhaled his masculine scent.

Before I was ready, he leaned back. "I'm sure Rihanna is

tired, too, but I'm betting she's not giving up. You have to think of your uncle and bringing closure to all of this mess."

I might have shot back a retort, but Jaxson was right. "Okay, let's do this. I still have to put the words to the arm movements."

We began again. For some reason, I was more relaxed and able to keep everything in sync for a change.

"You did it," he said.

"The arm part. Give me the paper so I can memorize the words."

"I have a better idea." Jaxson sat down at Drake's desk and typed in the spell. He then enlarged the words to make it look like a teleprompter. "There are seven arm configurations and seven phrases. I'm guessing that's how they are matched up. Give it a try."

The big print made it easy to see. "Because I might attract unwanted attention chanting the phrases out loud while swinging my arms, I'll say the spell to myself."

"You're the boss."

I glanced over at the table where I'd enjoyed many ice cream delights with Drake over the years, though of late, Jaxson had joined us. I pictured putting some kind of shield around it. If I couldn't create something that small, there was no way I'd be able to encircle an entire house.

As I read the words, I moved my arms. "Ugh."

"What happened?" Jaxson stopped scrolling the screen.

"I forgot what came next."

He calmly picked up the paper. "Where were you?"

"Between the fourth and fifth arm swing."

He told me what to do. "I remember now. Thanks. Let's

take it from the top."

For the next twenty minutes, I practiced and practiced. With each pass, I became more confident. When I made it through the arm movements and reciting the spell correctly, a crackling sounded off to my right.

When I looked toward the table, I saw nothing. No wait. Something shimmered. I stepped over to it and slowly punched the air above the table, but something hard stopped my fist.

I spun around. "Jaxson, Jaxson, check it out."

He came over and reached out. His fingers flattened on the invisible shield, and then his eyes widened. He turned toward me. "You did it!"

The next thing I knew, I was in his arms, and he was spinning me around. Joy at my success and at being with Jaxson shot my heartbeat up into the red zone. He set me down, and when we locked gazes, it was like the world stood still.

"Glinda Goodall, you are one amazing woman."

What happened next had only occurred in my dreams. Jaxson bent down and kissed me. His warm lips and gentle embrace altered something inside me—and that was a bit scary.

I stupidly broke the kiss, and then his mouth slightly parted. "I'm sorry. I thought…" he mumbled.

"You took me by surprise, that's all."

"I was just happy for your success," he said.

I wanted to ask if it meant anything more, but I didn't dare. Before I could figure out what to say, my cell buzzed, signaling a message. Perfect timing. "It's Rihanna. They're done."

Jaxson wore this cute little smug smile on his face, but I didn't even try to interpret it.

He handed me the spell. "You should practice every day until the heist goes down."

"Sound advice, partner."

I rushed out of the office and up the back staircase, trying to calm my heart. Jaxson Harrison had actually kissed me, and trust me, it was anything but plutonic.

Rihanna and Levy were standing next to the sofa. "How did it go?" I asked, though I suspected I was interfering in some kind of mutual share fest.

My cousin faced me. "Great! I can still only hear words and not full sentences, but I think I'm getting better."

"Don't let her fool you," Levy said. "I want to come back and get lessons from your cousin. There is strong innate talent there."

I looked over at Rihanna whose face had turned red. "I totally agree," I said. "And thank you, Levy, for helping out."

"Any time. I gave Rihanna my phone number in case she needs to send me a photo of someone to identify. I'm here to help. People like Winthrop give warlocks a bad name."

"I agree."

Just as Levy was about to leave, someone knocked on our office door. A second later, both Steve and Nash stepped inside. This was a surprise, but I had to guess it was about the next heist.

"Glinda, can we talk?" Steve asked.

"Is this about Winthrop?"

"It is."

"Levy here is the one who knows him."

"That's great. You're Gertrude's grandson then?"

"I am."

All three men shook hands. "I have news of the man who installed the safes in each of the homes that were robbed. Levy, could you stay for a moment and give us some idea what we might be up against?"

"It would be my pleasure."

I showed them to the sofa area while Rihanna rushed off to the kitchen, presumably to fix some tea or water.

"What did you learn?" I asked Steve.

"A man by the name of Eric Dunlap installed the safes for Emerson's. He was in every one of the houses that were robbed. Being the concerned sheriff that I am, I invited him to the precinct for a chat."

Jaxson smiled. "Told him you needed a safe, did you?"

Nash chuckled. "I see he knows you well, Sheriff."

"Actually, I asked for his help in solving this case."

I had to chuckle at that ploy. "How did that go over?"

"I was subtle. Trust me. I told him there had been a rash of robberies in the area by one man. I even showed him the photo of Winthrop, but Dunlap said he'd never seen him before."

"Do you have a photo of Dunlap with you?" Levy asked.

"I do. We have cameras almost everywhere in the office. I took a picture off the feed. It's a bit grainy, but you can see his face." Steve passed his phone to Levy.

He grunted. "His real name is Phil Dimitri. He's Winthrop's right-hand man. I've always suspected that they've pulled off capers together. While I have no proof, considering their extensive warlock skills, Phil probably gave Winthrop the locations of the safes as well the combinations. I imagine Winthrop did the actual theft while Phil was the lookout man."

"How did Winthrop know the safe numbers weren't changed?" Steve asked.

"I imagine he didn't. If at first you don't succeed, try, try again."

"That makes sense," I said. "If Winthrop was able to get in and out without breaking any windows or leaving the door unlocked, no one would be the wiser."

"That's my guess as well," Levy said.

"Two innocent men were tasered in the back and killed," Jaxson said. "Any idea which of the two culprits has that in their character?"

"My guess would be Dimitri. He's mean and ruthless. We kicked him out of the coven a long time ago because of his reckless behavior."

"Good to know," Steve said. "And Winthrop?"

"He never was in our coven, at least not since I've been a member."

"Thank you for your help."

Levy stood. "Rihanna has my number. Give me a call if you need anything else."

Steve stood too. "If you happen to hear of any robberies, let me or the Hampton River sheriff know."

"Will do."

Once Levy left, I wanted to tell them my good news. "While Rihanna was working with Levy on her mind reading skills, I—"

"You did it? You created a force field, didn't you?" My dear sweet cousin just spoiled my big surprise.

"You read my mind."

She grinned. "Guilty. Levy said I needed to practice as much as I can between now and when we get this guy." She looked over at Nash. "Don't be so surprised. I might be young, but I come from good witch stock."

He held up a hand. "I say more power to you."

For the next hour, the five of us honed our plan to take down this dangerous duo. The first step was to wait for the Hampton River sheriff to spot Winthrop heading someplace where Rihanna, Nash, and I could go and not look conspicuous. It was why I was hoping he'd pick a restaurant or a coffee shop.

"Glinda, are you sure you can erect this barrier around a whole house?" Steve asked.

"No, I can never be positive, but I'm going to give it my best try."

Steve smiled. "Good enough for me."

Chapter Sixteen

T WO DAYS LATER, after many practices, my cell rang at seven PM. It was Steve, and my heart pounded. "Did you find Winthrop?" My voice actually shook.

"Yes, but only because Dolly called Pearl."

My cell chimed, indicating someone had sent me a text. I was betting it was Dolly. "Don't tell me Winthrop is at the diner?"

"Yes, and she is saving you a booth, two seats away from him and his good friend, Eric or Phil or whatever name he's calling himself."

"Rihanna and I will head there now. Will Nash be there?"

"Yes, but only after you two are seated. Invite him to join you."

"I will. And thanks."

"No, thank you."

Pride filled me, as did a bit of unease. I was part of a real sting operation, one actually sanctioned by the sheriff's department. The moment I disconnected, I immediately responded to Dolly's text. I then called Rihanna.

"He's here, isn't he?" she asked.

I'll be honest. Her ability to know what I was about to say creeped me out. "You can read minds over the phone?"

"No, but Dolly messaged me, too."

That made sense. A knock sounded at my door. "Are you at my apartment?" I asked Rihanna.

"Yup."

I chuckled, swiped off my phone, and opened up. I almost didn't recognize my cousin in light blue jeans, a pretty red top and subdued makeup. With her hair swept up on top of her head in a messy bun, she was stunning. "Wow. I thought we were supposed to blend in. All eyes will be on you."

She blushed. "Thank you, but you need to change, too."

"While I do, why don't you head on over to the diner? Dolly has saved us a booth."

Iggy waddled up to us. "I'm coming. I can cloak myself and listen to everything."

I looked up at Rihanna. "Do you mind taking him?"

"Not at all, but can I just walk in with him?"

"No." I grabbed my large purse that was on the sofa. "Use this."

"Thanks."

As soon as Rihanna left with Iggy, I scrambled to put on my new attire. In all honesty, I was going to the diner merely for support. Nothing more. I couldn't read minds. In fact, it would be better if I wasn't at the diner in case Winthrop saw me outside of the house he wanted to rob. But it was too late to back out now.

I donned my new outfit, but I refused to check out my image in the mirror. I feared I might change my mind. I grabbed my phone and keys and rushed downstairs.

Once at the diner, I casually sauntered in to where Rihanna was sitting, not even glancing at the two criminals who were probably seated near the front. The only people behind Rihanna were either kids or older folk.

My cousin's back was to the men, so I slid in across from her. "I am so sorry I'm late." I made my announcement as loud as I dared.

"No problem. My uncle's not here yet."

Why was she pretending Nash was her uncle? I was sure she had her reasons.

"Yes, I do," she shot back without me saying a word. She smiled, and all I could do was shake my head.

"Where's my sidekick?" I whispered.

"Doing what he does best."

I figured that meant he was snooping. Never did I imagine fifteen years ago that I'd have a familiar who believed he was a detective.

Dolly came over with her pad in hand.

"What can I get you, ladies?"

I hadn't given thought to food, but I had to make my visit legitimate. "A grilled cheese with tomato and a sweet tea. Fries, of course."

Rihanna wasn't as familiar with the menu as I was. She'd probably need a minute unless she'd already looked it over. "How about a chocolate shake?"

"You got it."

"Can you do us a favor?" I asked Dolly. "Can you take a picture of me and my cousin?"

One brow rose, and then she seemed to understand. "Sure."

I slid in next to Rihanna and handed Dolly my phone.

She took aim. I thought it would be better than a selfie since she could include a larger view of the restaurant—including our two suspects. Click.

She smiled. "Got it."

"Thanks." I returned to my seat and then checked out the picture. She'd shot a four-second video. For one second, both men's faces were visible. Go, Dolly.

"This seat taken, ladies?" Nash said.

"Nope." Rihanna slid over.

With Nash's back to the men, he might be able to hear better. Not that I didn't trust Iggy, but I often feared his ability to remember everything was suspect.

I pretended to be interested in my phone so that both Nash and Rihanna could concentrate. Nash pulled out a small notepad from his top pocket, along with a pen. He was picking up habits from Steve.

He then slid the paper over to Rihanna. I wasn't sure what that was about, but Rihanna must have known. She scribbled what looked like an address, and my nerves flared. Was that where the next theft would occur? Were we finally going to catch the men who killed Uncle Lucas?

When Dolly came over and asked what Nash wanted to eat, he only ordered a cup of coffee.

Just as our meals arrived, Winthrop and his pal tossed down a bunch of cash on the table and left. I was quite thankful they didn't look our way. Apparently, we hadn't attracted attention.

Sharp claws crawled up my legs, and Iggy appeared. "That was exciting," he said.

I kind of doubted between Nash and Rihanna that Iggy

could add anything, but I wanted to hear him out. "Did you learn anything?" I whispered.

"Are you kidding? Of course, I did."

Iggy wasn't fond of people food, but since I hadn't ordered any lettuce, I broke a fry in half and gave it to him. "What did you learn?"

"Our sheriff scared that guy who was with Winthrop." Iggy continued with the rest of his news, and I then repeated it to Nash.

"Did he say why?" Nash asked.

"Sorry. Winthrop's friend thinks the cops are watching him. I got the sense he won't be joining Winthrop on the next heist. I'm not particularly happy about that if Dimitri was the one who tasered my uncle."

"We'll get him somehow. Anything else?"

I looked down at Iggy.

"Just that they are planning to break into some place that's in town here. The blond guy said the address so fast, I couldn't catch it."

"That's okay. Rihanna and Nash got it."

For once, Iggy said nothing. I looked at Rihanna. "Anything you'd like to add?"

"I had the sense that Winthrop would do this job and then cool it for a while. He seemed upset that Dimitri had spoken with Steve."

"If he hadn't, it would have looked more suspicious," Nash added.

"That's what Dimitri said."

I sipped my tea. "Then I guess we have our work cut out for us."

Everyone had their assignment. Jaxson would donate two bed sheets and gather the rope to nab them should Nash be able to grab a hold of the guy. Because these men were from Hampton River, I'm betting the sheriff there would help if necessary.

"What's the address?" I asked.

Nash rattled it off. Darn. It was about three miles from the center of town. "I guess Steve will be hiding inside to let me know when to erect the force field. Did they give a time?"

Nash shook his head and then looked over at Rihanna.

"I heard a few numbers. Some might have been the house number, but it's tomorrow. That's all I know."

I wasn't sure how much that helped. I snapped my fingers. "I have a hard time remaining invisible, but I'm wondering if perhaps Levy or someone he knows might be willing to follow Winthrop around for the day."

Rihanna smiled. "Let me give him a call."

I was about to suggest it might be more appropriate if I did it, but the two seemed to have a special bond. My cousin looked up and smiled. Listening into my thoughts was making me a bit uncomfortable, and I didn't care if she knew that.

"Levy?" she asked. "Yes, we made contact." She explained about the heist going down tomorrow. She told him that she knew the address but not the time of the heist. "We can't stake out the place all day long." She nodded. "For real? That would be great. Okay, I'll wait for your call."

"What did he say?" Nash asked as soon as she disconnected.

"He wants both men brought to justice. His coven will take turns tailing Winthrop—at least those capable of cloaking themselves."

That sounded great. "Did he ever say whether his kind can sense another warlock nearby, even if they are cloaked?"

"He never said, and I didn't think to ask him."

I waved a hand. "I trust Levy."

Nash's coffee arrived. "I hate to trouble you, but could I get this to go?"

"Sure thing, sweetie."

"I'll fill Steve in," Nash said. "He'll want to let the Hampton River sheriff's department know what's going to happen. We'll need to contact the homeowner and tell him to vacate the house—for his own safety. We already have the counterfeit bills that are scented with something I'm particularly sensitive to. If I get within ten feet of the guy, I'll be able to find him."

If the next home targeted was in Witch's Cove, then Jaxson—and not some Hampton River deputy—would be hiding nearby, ready to toss on the sheet and wrap the thief in rope. Steve said he wasn't sure it was legal to have a civilian help, but Jaxson reminded him that this was no ordinary heist, and Steve finally agreed.

While Nash and Jaxson were trying to subdue this guy, it was my job to create this force field that would stop the thief from leaving the premises. How long I could keep a whole house surrounded was anyone's guess. I'd not tried the spell on a large area, but hopefully, I could do it.

After Nash left the diner, we finished our meal. I called Jaxson to let him know that the plan was on for tomorrow.

"In that case, I'm going to spend the night at the office. I have a sleeping bag and an air mattress."

I sensed some anxiety, but I wasn't sure why. "Because?"

"Who's to say Winthrop didn't recognize you two at the diner? I can't imagine wearing different clothes would disguise both of you all that much. He might want to tie up loose ends, especially if he saw you during the memorial service."

My stomach nearly revolted. I hadn't thought of that. And here I'd made kind of a spectacle of myself when I came in. What had I been thinking? "Thank you."

"No problem. Rihanna is family."

"Then I owe you."

He chuckled. "Does that mean you'll be willing to go out to dinner with me sometime?"

We went out all the time, but I sensed this was like a formal date. Butterflies attacked my gut, but I wanted to see where this relationship could go. "I am."

"I'll meet you back at the office when you're done eating."

"Okay." I disconnected.

"Don't tell me," Rihanna said. "Jaxson is worried."

"Did you read my mind?"

"No, I could hear the conversation. He talks kind of loud."

I smiled. "He does at that."

Iggy crawled up on my lap, clearly wanting to go. I finished my dinner and paid. Since we had to pass the office on the way to my apartment, she didn't complain that we went together. However, when I started up the steps, she faced me.

"I'm good."

"I'm sure you are, but I'm not. Jaxson is expecting me back at the office. Besides, I'd like him to escort me home."

She grinned. "My bad. Come on."

Upstairs, I found Jaxson blowing up his air mattress. He put the plug in it. "Everything go okay?"

I chuckled. "No one attacked us as we walked here, if that is what you're asking."

"But you could have been followed."

That was unsettling. "Yes." I looked at what he'd brought to the office. "What's with the flour?"

He shrugged. "You know. In case some invisible man manages to get by me, I want to be ready."

"That would shock him. Not to mention, it would cause a coughing fit."

Jaxson tapped his temple. "I'm smart that way."

"Yes, you are." I turned to Rihanna. "Your protector will be back shortly, assuming I can convince him to escort me back to my place."

"Of course." He faced Rihanna. "I'd suggest you lock the door after us, but I don't think that will do much good," Jaxson said.

"Good point. I'll put a chair under the doorknob. That's what they do in the movies. Let's hope he's not an expert in telekinesis. If I hear any jiggling of the lock, I'll call 9-1-1."

Jaxson smiled. "Perfect. I'll knock three times to let you know it's me."

"I'll be fine."

I was sure she would be. Rihanna was turning out to be highly resourceful. Jaxson and I left. As soon as we reached the bottom of the steps, he wrapped a protective arm around my waist. While I couldn't sense his worry, that action implied it.

"We're going to be fine," I said.

"I know, but things can always go wrong, especially when

witches and warlocks are involved."

"Meaning?"

"We don't know if these guys can do a spell to cancel your spell."

Yikes, I hadn't thought of that. If Winthrop recognized me—and why wouldn't he?—he might decide to use me as a human shield.

At least, Rihanna had promised to stay in the car during the robbery. She was acting as not only our getaway driver, but as our videographer. It might be the only way to prove anything in court.

When we entered the Tiki Hut Grill, Jaxson insisted on following me up the stairs. "If I could be in two places at once, I'd sleep in front of your door, too, you know."

"I do, and thank you." I stood on my tiptoes and kissed him quickly.

Iggy popped his head out of my bag. "Knock it off, you guys."

That cracked both of us up. Jaxson winked. "Sleep well, Glinda."

That was so not going to happen.

Chapter Seventeen

I WAS A mess from the moment I woke up, until the time Rihanna received the call from Levy regarding the heist. She'd gone to school—against her wishes, mind you—but I told her I'd call the school to say she might be needed at a moment's notice.

In the end, I never had to call, because Levy didn't contact her until about an hour after she got home.

"What time is this going down?" she asked her new mentor. "Okay. Thanks, Levy."

She swiped off the phone. "Someone, wink, wink, must have let it slip that the homeowners just left town, so Winthrop will be robbing the place tonight. Levy believes the theft will occur around nine."

"I'll call Steve and tell him to rally the troops."

"I've already loaded the car with the sheets and rope," Jaxson said. He'd been quietly working at his computer, and I wasn't sure he was paying attention. Apparently, I was wrong.

I smiled and then patted my pocket. "I have my spell, but I swear if I forget one line or one arm swing, I'll hang up this witch stuff."

"You'll do great," he said.

Jaxson was always Mr. Supportive. "I'm hoping I won't be

needed, because Nash will get close enough to smell the money and then nab the guy."

"I'll be ready whatever happens," Jaxson said.

"I know you will be." I looked over at Rihanna. "Even though you will be in the car, I think your usual attire might be best."

"I was planning on it. And you?"

"I'll stand out too much in pink. I need to go low key since I'll be on the sidewalk. The last thing I need is to attract attention. It will be bad enough that I'll look like some crazy person swinging my arms around and mumbling to myself."

Jaxson smiled. "Nice image. But speaking of sidewalks, what do you say we do a drive by to see if they have one? For all we know, the house is surrounded by an eight-foot tall cement wall."

"That would be bad."

"Tell me about it. I also need to scope out the possible escape routes this guy might take, in order to ensure your shield will be sufficient. We have to decide where the best place would be to park."

"I'm game." I turned to Rihanna. "You want to come, right?"

"Are you kidding? Of course. I'll shoot some photos so we can study them when we get back."

"Good. It's why we didn't check out the place this morning. We need you." I was liking how well the three of us worked together as a team. "And don't you dare say you agree. You're creeping me out with all this mind reading stuff."

She laughed. "I'll try not to read your mind, but come on, you are an open book."

Jaxson grabbed his keys. "Don't look at me. Rihanna is right."

"So everyone keeps telling me."

He looked at both of us. "I trust one of you has the address?"

"I do," Rihanna said. "I've already programmed it into the app on my phone."

Iggy pranced up to us. "I'm coming with you."

Since we probably would stay in the car, I saw no reason for him not to join us. I leaned down and lifted him onto my shoulder. It was his favorite way to travel.

The trip to the targeted house only took a few minutes. Thankfully, it had no fence. Score one for us. Jaxson pulled to the curb. "There's a sidewalk, which is good."

I visualized performing my ritual. "I'll stand in front of the car. That way if I need to get to safety, I can."

"Good thinking."

Jaxson studied the neighborhood. "There are lots of places for this guy to hide." He pointed to the area between the two houses. "It looks like an alley. If he heads back there, he'll be gone for good."

"I'm guessing he'll have a bike, but once he jumps on it, both of them will disappear."

"That will be a problem," Jaxson said.

"Even if Steve signals the Hampton River sheriff's department when it's time to block off the streets, it might do no good."

"Then let's hope your plan works, Glinda."

"My plan? We all had input. I don't want the responsibility if this goes south."

"And if it succeeds?" Jaxson asked.

"In that case..." I laughed.

"That's what I thought." Jaxson started the engine and took off for home.

These next few hours were going to be some of the longest ones of my life.

JAXSON KNOCKED ON Rihanna's bedroom door. "It's time to go, ladies. We want to get there before Winthrop does."

I looked over at Rihanna who was putting finishing touches on her eye makeup—something I thought was unnecessary considering she wouldn't be getting out of the car. I was not going to upset her by commenting, however. "Do I look like I blend in?" I asked.

"Kind of." She pulled open her dresser drawer and took out a thin black shirt. "Put this on. I like your mint green top, but you'll be really easy to see, even in the dark."

I put on the proffered shirt. The arms were a little long, but that was okay. "Thanks."

It was now or never. We stepped out. Rihanna had her camera slung over her shoulder, and I had my spell.

I motioned to Iggy. "Come on, champ."

He crawled up my leg and then climbed to my shoulder via my arm. "Let's do this."

My familiar made me laugh. "Remember, if you talk, they can understand you."

"I wasn't born yesterday."

At times, it seemed like it. We'd done everything we

could to prepare for this moment. Steve had dropped off the earpieces a few hours ago that we were to use to communicate with everyone on the team. I turned mine on and placed it in my ear. Jaxson and Rihanna activated theirs, too.

"We're on our way to the house, Steve," I said after tapping the earpiece.

"Roger that. I'm inside already, and Nash is lurking outside. The Hampton River sheriff's department is on standby down the street."

If Rihanna or Nash had misunderstood the address, everyone would have gone to a lot of trouble for nothing. Not to mention how scared the poor homeowners must be right now wondering if their house might be destroyed by the thieves. Thankfully, the Dixon family was willing to stay away from their house until tomorrow.

Jaxson drove, but Rihanna would be ready to drive us out of there should the need arise.

About a half a block from the home, Jaxson stopped the car and slipped out since he needed to hide nearby. Rihanna moved over to the driver's seat and continued toward the house.

Fingers crossed that Winthrop's partner didn't show up and ask what I was doing here. My only thought was to say I was considering buying a home in the neighborhood and wanted to scope out the area at night to see if it was safe. That was weak, but I couldn't come up with anything better.

Rihanna pulled to a stop one house away from where we believed the thief would strike.

"Now we wait," I said.

There was no use in me standing outside and being seen

until after the thief had gone inside. That would be my cue to get ready with the arm symphony I had to perform. Was I nervous? Yes, but I had to stay calm and believe in my magic in order for it to succeed.

I didn't see either Jaxson or Nash for that matter. I would have used my earpiece to ask if Jaxson was okay, but I didn't need him to talk and give away his position should the thief be invisible and roaming about.

"A bike just appeared," Nash whispered over my coms.

I jerked to attention. This implied that Winthrop was on his way to the house. Steve and everyone else would be on high alert.

I inhaled deeply. "Wish me luck," I said to Rihanna.

"You don't need it. Go make that shield."

I loved her confidence. Once the front door opened and then closed, I eased out of the car. I had no idea how long it would take for Winthrop to open the safe and grab the cash. I also didn't know how long a large shield would last once it was erected. The small shields I'd tried lasted about two minutes, but I had no idea what one that covered half an acre would do.

Steve had told us that when we heard three taps over our earpiece, followed by one tap, it meant the safe had been opened. From there, it would probably take no longer than a minute to grab the cash, stuff it in a sack of some kind, and leave. Winthrop had unlocked the front door in seconds; I doubted it would take him any longer on the way out.

As much as I wanted to shift from side to side to bleed off some excess energy, I forced myself to stand still and focus on the upcoming task.

Tap, tap, tap. My pulse soared. Tap.

This was it. For a split second, I forgot the first phrase, but then it came to me. I mentally recited each phrase slowly as I did my intricate arm movements. If I had been holding some kind of stick with a ribbon attached to the end, I would have done well in a competition.

The front door opened. Here goes!

I did the final arm swing and waited for the shield to form. Between the moonlight and front porch lights, I should be able to detect it.

Only nothing happened, and panic gripped my insides. He was going to get away, and I couldn't let that happen— not for those who'd been burglarized nor for Uncle Lucas' family.

Feet pounded. Out of sheer desperation, I clasped the stone on my necklace, praying this man would be caught. Instead of some inner voice telling me what to do, the ghost of my Nana floated in front of me, and her appearance shocked me out of my stupor.

"Stop feeling sorry for yourself. You're a grown woman. Suck it up and concentrate. Imagine that shield now!"

With that she disappeared. I was stunned, but seeing her again renewed my determination to succeed. I had maybe three seconds to do this. I focused on the south side of the property, because that was where I'd seen the man's bike.

Nash was in the yard, and he too was heading south. Using all of my concentration, I repeated the last arm swing.

Boom! A body materialized and tumbled backward onto his butt. The urge to yell out that I'd done it was strong, but I clamped a hand over my mouth.

Nash grabbed him. "Jaxson, get over here!"

Out of nowhere, Jaxson appeared, carrying the sheet. He threw it over the man. Between him and Nash, they managed to wrap the rope around him, and relief rushed through me.

"Got him," came Nash's voice over my com.

I kept my gaze on the three men. I didn't trust the warlock not to have some trick in mind, though I bet he hadn't expected to have someone put up a force field around the house. They better keep him covered since I didn't need him to see me and realize I helped ruin his little scam.

A Hampton River deputy rushed up the sidewalk, and as soon as he tried to step on the lawn to help, he stopped and rubbed his head.

"What in the world?" he mumbled.

Whoops! "Is it safe to take down the shield?" I asked using the coms.

"Yes, Glinda. And thank you," Nash said.

In the past, the shield just disappeared. I grabbed my Nana's necklace once more and mentally asked her for some words of wisdom.

"Just relax."

I swear her words entered my mind, because I didn't see her image again. When I did as she said, the shield disintegrated, allowing Nash and Jaxson to escort the thief down the road to their car.

The poor deputy who ran into the nearly invisible shield probably thought it had been some bird smashing into him. Explaining about invisible men and force fields might have been too much for him to grasp right now.

I turned around and slipped into the front seat of the car.

"Did you get the capture on tape?"

Rihanna grinned. "I sure did."

"Great." I tapped my com. "Jaxson, are you riding with us?"

"No, you ladies go ahead. I'll meet you back at the office."

"Okay."

It was probably better that Nash and Steve have the extra help. I still worried that something might go wrong. Warlocks were tricky beasts.

Steve came out of the house, locked up, and then headed toward his cruiser. With our jobs finished, I removed my coms, as did Rihanna.

She started the engine. "Do you think we'll ever find proof who killed my dad?"

"Good question. I'm hoping there will be evidence some-where of Phil Dimitri's involvement in all of this, assuming he was the one who tasered both men. It's possible that Winthrop will give up his friend for a reduced sentence. Even if he didn't hold the taser, he is still guilty of murder."

Iggy crawled up the back of the car seat and onto my shoulder. "That was fun. You're a real witch now."

"Whatever are you talking about? I've always been a witch. Don't forget my spell is what enables Jaxson to talk to you."

He settled in on my shoulder. "I guess."

I wasn't going to let Iggy spoil my good mood. "Rihanna, if you plan on writing up what happened here tonight for a school project, would you pass it by the sheriff first? I don't know if you can say anything until after the trial."

"Trials take months. I probably will have graduated by

then." Her slightly depressed tone was mixed with some cheer, probably because we had caught the thief—in large part to her intel.

"There is that."

When we arrived back at the office, she parked and then faced me. "If Winthrop can open locks with his mind, what is to prevent him from opening the cell door lock?"

My chest tightened. "I don't know. Let's hope the sheriff has a work around for that. Chain Winthrop to the floor perhaps? Though I suppose he could open that lock, too."

"You think the sheriff's department has restraints like that?"

"If he doesn't, he should. This is Witch's Cove, after all. No telling what some of the residents are capable of."

"You are so right."

I could only hope I wasn't right in this case. The last thing we needed was for Winthrop to escape.

Chapter Eighteen

WHEN JAXSON RETURNED to the office, he looked tired but excited at the same time. In his hands was a bag from the Tiki Hut Grill.

Rihanna nodded to the sack. "Anything special inside?"

I didn't think she was the type who needed sweets. On second thought, she had swiped up that pastry pretty fast and then wanted an ice cream sundae.

"Yes. I bought us some celebration cookies." Jaxson turned to me. "How about cracking open that bottle of wine that you bought a while ago?"

I wasn't sure that was a good idea since Rihanna couldn't join us.

"I'll have some tea." She looked over at me and smiled.

I would never get used to her reading my mind. "Great. Jax, how about you open the bottle while I get the glasses. Come on, Rihanna."

Once in the tiny kitchen, we gathered the glasses, her tea, and some plates. When we came out, Jaxson had the bottle open. He poured us a glass and then opened the bag of cookies.

I held up my glass. "To a great team."

"To a great team," both said in unison.

The first sip was divine. As much as I wanted to shout for joy, I had so many questions. "Do we know for sure that our thief was Steward Winthrop?" I asked.

"He was."

"When Steve asked about his partner, I imagine he claimed he always worked alone?"

"Two for two."

"Did you learn if the Hampton River sheriff's office plans to get a warrant to search Winthrop's house for the stolen goods?"

"Three for three. They are in the process of getting them, but in the meantime, they have Winthrop's house under surveillance in case his partner shows up there or back at his house. Dimitri might have figured out something went wrong when Winthrop didn't contact him, and we're hoping he decides to gather their previously stolen goods."

"Let's hope, though it's possible Dimitri was at the house and watched the whole thing go down," I added.

Rihanna grabbed a cookie. "We should have asked Levy to come with us. He might have been able to sense if another warlock was close by."

"Too late now, but I would have thought you'd have that skill," I said.

"I might, but I'm thinking sitting in the car would have blocked my abilities."

"Maybe."

"Ladies, how about we celebrate the moment? Let's be happy that the thief is behind bars, and that what he stole will be recovered—or at least a lot of it."

"You don't think he would have pawned it already?" I

asked.

"I wouldn't have," Jaxson said. "A smart thief would drive to a different county and sell the stuff in several pawn shops once the heat died down."

"He could have used a professional fence," Rihanna said.

"Professional fence? What kind of television shows have you been watching?"

She just smiled.

It was already quite late, and Rihanna should be in bed. Before I could suggest we call it a night, my cell rang. I checked the caller ID. "It's Steve."

"Put him on speaker," Rihanna said.

"Hey, Steve. Rihanna and Jaxson are listening in."

"Great. I wanted to say thank you all for your help. Without the shield, we would have lost Winthrop for sure."

I was about to say that Nash could have shifted into a wolf and followed the scent, but I hadn't brought up the concept of werewolves to Rihanna yet. "You're welcome."

"I don't want you guys to worry about Winthrop escaping. I called Levy and asked if he could put a spell on the jail lock to prevent our thief from opening it."

I smiled. "That's very clever of you to fight fire with fire, so to speak."

"Why, thank you."

"Any news on his partner-in-crime?" Jaxson asked.

"Not yet, but don't worry. We'll find the guy who killed Rihanna's dad."

That was all that mattered—that and retrieving the stolen goods. "Thank you." I hung up. "We might get closure after all," I said.

Rihanna smiled. "I hope so."

After Jaxson and I finished our glass of wine, I corked the bottle. "When justice has been served, we can finish this."

"I like that. Come on. I'll walk you home," Jaxson said.

"Not that I mind, but I'm good. Winthrop is behind bars."

He dipped his chin. "Glinda."

"Of course. What am I thinking? Dimitri is not. If he has any idea Rihanna or I had anything to do with his capture, he might want revenge."

"Yes, which is why I am once more staying here with Rihanna."

"I have an idea," my cousin said.

"Yes?"

"How about the three of us stay at Glinda's place? I can take the sofa and Jaxson, you can use your sleeping bag."

I wished I could read her mind, but from the way her fingers were fidgeting, she'd feel safer if we all stayed together. "That sounds wonderful."

I for one probably wouldn't sleep a wink knowing Jaxson was right outside my door.

IT WASN'T UNTIL about four the next day that Steve showed up at the office. I figured he'd waited until Rihanna returned from school to deliver any news. After all, it was her father who'd been murdered.

"Did you find something?" I asked.

"We did. Is Rihanna here?"

"Yes, I'll get her."

Jaxson offered the sheriff something to drink, but he declined.

I was about to knock on Rihanna's door, when she opened it up. She must have heard us talking. "The sheriff is here?"

"Yes. He might have something for us."

Jaxson, Rihanna, and I joined Steve.

"I just heard from the sheriff over at Hampton River. He pulled some strings and got two search warrants, one for Winthrop's house and the other for Dimitri's. They found about half of the stolen goods at Winthrop's place, but not much of the money. They're going to compare his bank deposits with that of what was stolen to see if he left a money trail—not that we need it for a conviction."

"What about Dimitri? He was the one I always thought killed Uncle Lucas."

"They found a taser at his house, as well as Mrs. Holt's necklace."

"Yes! She will be so happy."

"I called her and told her already. She was thrilled. Mrs. Holt was going to go over to Hampton River to give a positive identification. Since she had a photo of the items from her safe, there should be no problem with her getting everything back after the trial."

"I am so happy for her."

"Were you able to compare the taser to the marks on the two…" Jaxson probably didn't want to discuss details in front of Rihanna.

"It's okay," she said. "I can take it."

Steve nodded. "We asked the first medical examiner to compare the two marks. When he is finished, I'll have Dr. Sanchez do the same, but I'm betting the weapon will be a match."

"I trust the sheriff over there is going to bring Dimitri in and hold him for murder and theft?"

"He is. Even if the guy somehow weasels his way out of any of the crimes, I think we can get Winthrop to talk. He's just as guilty of murder as Dimitri. He'll be facing life imprisonment, too."

"Good. I hope you asked Levy to visit the jail in Hampton River so he can do his magic there," Rihanna said.

"I did. Don't worry. You ladies are safe from either man—not that they know you were involved."

His words made all the knots in my stomach disappear. "That is so great to hear."

Steve stood. Jaxson did too, and then he shook the sheriff's hand. "I enjoyed working with you guys."

"All three of you were a great help. You will be forever my witchy-go-to team."

We all laughed. "Let's hope there won't be a next time for a long time. Right now, I'd be happy spying on cheating husbands and locating lost dogs," I said.

"Dream on, Glinda." Steve turned to Rihanna. "Thanks for sending me the video. I'm not sure if a jury will believe that a person can disappear, but I'll let the judge decide. Considering these men's extensive powers, we might transport them to our other court system that deals with such things."

I believe he was referring to the court that had dealt with the werewolves in the past. "That would be great," I said, hoping Rihanna wasn't paying attention to what I was thinking.

"I'll talk it over with Nash."

With that, the sheriff left. I turned to Rihanna. "How are you feeling about all this? Do you think it will give you any closure knowing who killed your dad—assuming the doctors prove the taser found in Dimitri's house killed him?"

"Not really. Sure, I want justice, but I'll never see him again. That's why it's so painful."

"I hear you, but I'm betting with some practice, you might be able to contact him."

"You think?"

"I would talk to your Aunt Wendy. She's the expert."

"Can I ask her now?"

I laughed. "I don't see why not."

With more pep than I'd seen her show in a while, she hurried off.

"She seems to be embracing her witch side quite well," Jaxson said once Rihanna had left.

"Totally, and for that I'm glad. I think it's where she needs to be."

"Thinking about where we need to be, what about that dinner date?"

"I would love to, but I have an idea."

"Tell me," he said.

"Rihanna asked the Witch's Cove museum to have an exhibition of her dad's photos this weekend. How about if we combine the showing with dinner? We'll make it a special night."

Jaxson wrapped his arms around my waist and pulled me close. "I like the way you think."

Before he could kiss me, someone knocked on our door.

The timing couldn't have been worse. "Come in."

It was Mrs. Holt with a smile on her face. "I just came over to thank you two. The sheriff at Hampton River told me how much you two did to recover my necklace."

"You're welcome." As much as I wanted to find the necklace, my dedication in this case was more about learning who had murdered my uncle.

She handed Jaxson a check. "Once more, thank you. I will be sure to tell my neighbors how great you guys were to work with."

That compliment boosted my spirits. Okay, the check boosted our dwindling bank account, too. "Thank you, so much."

When she left, I wasn't sure what to do. "With our client satisfied, where do we go from here?"

"Are you talking about The Pink Iguana Sleuths or us?"

Butterflies attacked my stomach. "I was talking about our business."

"Uh-huh." He smiled. "In that case, we need to work on our marketing plan. Word of mouth is good, but we need to remind people about what we do."

"And we don't just do murders either."

He smiled. "I think it's fair to say we are willing to do things that don't involve a murder, but somehow someone ends up dead."

"It does seem like we get involved in them. I remember the days when nothing like this ever happened in Witch's Cove."

"Times change," he said.

Boy, do they ever.

Chapter Nineteen

A few days later

AT THE PHOTOGRAPHY exhibit, my cousin was surrounded by quite a few of her high school friends, as well as one very cute male—Gavin Sanchez. Rihanna had aptly named the showing: The world through the eyes of the soul. She'd picked that because she had said her father could see straight into a person's soul, and I couldn't agree more.

Jaxson, who looked very handsome in his navy-blue suit, leaned over. "This is a great turnout."

"It is. And here I was afraid the locals wouldn't be that interested in art."

"Didn't you say Aunt Fern had a hand in the promotion?" he asked.

I smiled. "She did. She and her friends put the word out, and I'm actually surprised it's not standing room only in here."

He laughed. "Speaking of which, where is Aunt Fern?"

We had offered to drive her, but she said she didn't need a lift. I figured she might want to come over with Pearl, Dolly, or the Daniel sisters.

The door opened, and who should come in but my aunt. I nudged Jaxson. "Take a look at her."

Aunt Fern was dressed in a rather elegant salmon colored knee length dress, adorned with a rhinestone belt and a matching necklace. She looked amazing and, dare I say, sexy?

He whistled. "She looks great."

A tall, strikingly good-looking gray-haired man entered right behind her. He had on a black suit, light gray shirt, and a muted red tie. He placed a hand on my aunt's waist. What? Where had he come from?

"I think my aunt has been holding out on me," I said.

"You didn't know she was dating someone?"

"No, and neither Iggy nor Aimee ever said a word. Let's saunter over and say hello."

"You mean you want to spy on her?" Jaxson said.

I stuck my tongue out at him. "Of course."

We had to weave our way through the crowd to reach her.

"Glinda. Jaxson. I'd like you to meet Peter Upton."

I didn't need Rihanna's ability to read her mind. I could tell my aunt was gloating. I held out my hand. "I'm Glinda Goodall, her niece."

Jaxson introduced himself as my business partner. I shouldn't be disappointed in his designation since we hadn't discussed us being anything other than that despite those wonderful kisses.

"Great to meet you both. Fern has told me so much about you."

"How long have you two been dating?" Was that tacky of me to ask? Yes, but my own aunt should have filled me in.

After the last disaster with that jerky boyfriend, Bob, I was glad she was willing to give it another go.

"About three weeks." He turned to my aunt. "Right,

dear?"

Dear? I would ask Jaxson to do a quick check on the guy to make sure he was on the up and up.

"Yes, but it's been wonderful and so much fun that it seems like it's been a lifetime."

Really? Talk about tacky.

My aunt did a quick visual scan of the room. "This exhibition looks amazing. Where's Rihanna?" my aunt asked. "I want to congratulate her on getting this organized so quickly."

"She did an amazing job. I'm so happy that she had the opportunity to know her dad before he passed." More like murdered. I looked for her and spotted her coming out of another room. "Rihanna is over there." I pointed in her direction.

The two of them headed to the wall of photos.

We'd already congratulated Rihanna on setting this up. From the smile on my cousin's face, she'd really found her place here in Witch's Cove.

"Glinda?" said a deep male voice.

I spun around. "Levy?"

"Don't be so surprised. Even us wacky warlocks can enjoy art."

"I didn't mean that."

"I know. I wanted to see how Rihanna was doing." He looked around. When he spotted her, he smiled. "She looks happy."

"She is, and a large part is thanks to you."

"You're making me blush. Without her willingness and abilities, those two thieves wouldn't have been caught. Our coven thanks both of you. They were a disgrace to our kind. If you ever need anything, don't hesitate to call."

"We will." I could use all the help I could get.

"I'm going to check out these photos. I regret never having met the great Lucas Samuels," Levy said.

"Me, too. At least, not in the last fifteen years."

He rubbed my arm. "I know."

Jaxson placed a hand on my back. "Ready to go to dinner?"

"I am."

Before we could reach the door, we were stopped a few more times by well-wishers. Just as Jaxson pulled open the door, Rihanna rushed up to us. "Glinda, Jaxson. Guess who came?"

I was about to say Levy, but the man next to her was in a uniform. "Tell me."

"This was dad's boss."

He held out his hand. "Commander Daniel Fernandez."

"Commander." I swallowed hard.

He handed Rihanna an envelope. "I came to deliver this in person. When Lucas signed up fifteen years ago, he signed a paper giving his daughter and former wife his retirement benefits should he pass. This should be enough to secure both of their futures."

"Really?" Rihanna said. "Wow."

Wow was right. First, Uncle Lucas leaves her and my aunt his condo and now this? "What a nice surprise." I wasn't sure what else to say.

"I heard that Rihanna inherited her father's talents."

Oh, no. I didn't like where this was going. "She did, but she plans on being a photojournalist."

He smiled. "I think that would be great, but if she changes her mind, the country would be proud to embrace her."

I'm sure they would, but I hoped Rihanna had sense not to want the dangerous life her father led. Besides, she needed to be a kid for a few more years.

Gavin moved next to Rihanna. "Everything okay?"

She looked up at him as if she was star-struck. Oh, boy. "Everything is great," she said.

Jaxson pressed a hand on my back. "Come on, Glinda. Let's leave them alone."

Jaxson knew me well.

I thanked the Commander for coming all this way to deliver the news in person.

"My pleasure. I want to check out Lucas' work, and then I'll be heading back."

I didn't ask to where.

The outside air was balmy and rather humid, but I wouldn't trade Witch's Cove for anywhere else in the world. Jaxson opened his car door and waited for me to get in. Back in high school, I bet he never opened a door for anyone. How nice that he'd changed.

Even though I'd been out to eat a million times with him, this was our first official date, and I was actually nervous. Finding killers almost seemed easy compared to this.

He slipped into the driver's side. "I found a nice restaurant in Hampton River I thought we should try."

"Really? Hampton River?"

"Why not? I thought you'd feel right at home being in a town full of warlocks and witches."

Witch's Cove had a lot of those, too. However, I had

spent most of my life only wearing pink and living in the same town. When I put on normal clothes, I didn't shrivel up and die. Maybe it was time to stretch my wings a little. "Sounds like a great idea."

As we headed out of town, my mind was not on the wonderful meal we would have or the great potential conversation, but on the kiss that would seal the end to a perfect night.

I hope you enjoyed seeing how Glinda, Jaxson, and Rihanna use magic to help find the murderer. Book 7, The Pink Iguana Sleuth company, comes in time for Halloween, but the festivities are marred by yet another death. Did you expect anything less?

A Pink Pumpkin Party (book 7 of A Witch's Cove Mystery) is available.

Buy on Amazon or read for FREE on Kindle Unlimited

Don't forget to sign up for my Cozy Mystery newsletter to learn about my discounts and upcoming releases. If you prefer to only receive notices regarding my releases, follow me on BookBub.
http://smarturl.it/VellaDayNL
bookbub.com/authors/vella-day

Here is a sneak peek.

"YOU WANT *ALL* of the pumpkins painted pink?" Rihanna asked.

I chuckled at her horror. "Are you suggesting a few get a splash of black?"

"You know that Halloween should have more representation than just pink," my cousin said with a teenage rebellious tone.

I understood where she was coming from. Halloween was synonymous with orange and black. "Fine. We can have some unpainted orange ones and a few black ones."

Rihanna grinned. "You are the best."

I chuckled. "Keep painting."

Let me explain my cousin's comment—and my response. First of all, my name is Glinda Goodall, named after the movie character Glinda, the Good Witch from the South, and I live in Witch's Cove, Florida, a small beach town full of witches, psychics, fortune tellers, and a few werewolves tossed in for good measure.

After deciding that being a math teacher wasn't my thing, I moved home and took a job as a waitress in my aunt's restaurant, the Tiki Hut Grill. All was well for a few years until Jaxson Harrison, the brother of my best male friend, Drake, returned to town. Jaxson was hot—as in great to look at but also hot-headed. No doubt about it, our newcomer was definitely trouble.

When our deputy was murdered, Jaxson became our number one suspect since he'd just finished serving three years in jail for supposedly robbing a liquor store. Naturally, I had to help Drake prove his brother wasn't the killer.

That intervention led to a series of events that ended with me and Jaxson starting The Pink Iguana Sleuths. Shock, I know. To be honest, I can't keep my nose out of anything, and as it turns out, I'm actually quite good at solving murder cases—with the help of our sheriff's department, of course. I lucked out, because Jaxson was a genius when it came to doing research. I swear the man could find anything on the computer. Oh, yeah. If you haven't guessed, Jaxson wasn't guilty of any crime. He'd been framed.

So, what did this history lesson have to do with painting

Halloween pumpkins pink? And why was my eighteen-year old cousin helping me?

That was easy. Except when duty calls—that is, when I'm on a case—I only wear pink, which was why I was painting the pumpkins that distinctive color. However, Rihanna only wears black since she has a need to express herself, too. As for why my eighteen-year old cousin was helping me instead of being back in Tallahassee where she lived? Once more, simple. After years of drug abuse, Rihanna's mother finally decided to enter rehab, which meant my cousin needed a place to stay for a few months. After some debate, she moved here. She's now living in a room off of our office. And by *our office*, I mean the one I share with my business partner—turned potential boyfriend—Jaxson. Can you understand why I had to fill you in? My life is complicated.

I'm glad she's here, because Rihanna is quite a talented psychic. In fact, in the two months since her arrival, my cousin has helped solve a few crimes.

"Did you finish the vampire for the coffin?" she asked.

"Almost." My parents own the funeral home that sits next to the Tiki Hut Grill where tomorrow night's party will be held. "I'm still working on the face. I've made it out of papier-mâché, and I just need to paint the fangs and eyes."

"Cool. And the graveyard?"

I was impressed that my cousin had been listening to my plans to make this the best Halloween party ever. "I'm using the same gravestones we used last year. They're made out of Styrofoam, but they look real."

Rihanna grabbed a pink pumpkin whose paint had dried and added black eyeliner, long eyelashes, and black lips. I—

the woman who loved pink—was willing to admit that her artwork improved the pink pumpkin greatly.

My cell rang. "It's Jaxson."

He and his brother, Drake, were in charge of renting and then setting up the projector that would splash the image of ghosts on the restaurant ceiling. Tomorrow, my father would get his crew to carry over the coffin with the vampire inside.

My body sagged at all that needed to be done by then. I don't know why I had allowed my Aunt Fern to talk me into doing this again this year. Sure, Halloween—and maybe Christmas—were my favorite holidays, but it took a lot out of me to make this *the* event of the year.

Thankfully—or not so thankfully—in the last month, no one had been murdered in Witch's Cove, which meant I had the time to devote to this endeavor.

That didn't mean Jaxson and I had no clients. We'd been hired to follow one husband to see why he came home late two days a week. Naturally, the wife was convinced he was having an affair. Was he? No. Turned out, he was taking dance lessons to surprise her on their anniversary. Was that sweet or what?

And then there was case of the stolen wedding gown. In that instance, the woman's twenty-two-year-old daughter had forgotten to tell her mother that she needed to lend it to her best friend for her wedding.

As much as these small jobs brought in some needed cash, it didn't give me the rush that a good old-fashioned murder did. However, if too many people died in Witch's Cove, our tourism rate might go down.

"I'm done," Rihanna announced.

"Great." We were sitting in the alley between the Tiki Hut Grill and The Cove Mortuary. Not wanting anyone to come by and steal our fine artwork, I had waited until the pumpkins had almost dried before moving them inside. "I'm going to carry the rest of these to the storage room."

"I'll wait here."

"Thanks." One by one, I placed the finished masterpieces on one of the cleared storage room shelves.

When I returned, Rihanna had gathered the remaining supplies. "What did you finally decide to wear for the party?" she asked.

I had gone back and forth many times, but the costume shop in town had limited choices, and I didn't want to ask my Aunt Fern to make me one. I'd done that too many times in the past. "I'm going as Supergirl, and Jaxson will be Superman."

"Ooh. I'd like to see that man in a tight outfit."

"Rihanna Samuels. No lustful thoughts. Besides, you have your own cutie to watch."

Heat raced up her face. "I do at that."

"What are you and Gavin going as?"

She shrugged. "I had thought about wearing a Fairy costume with blue wings and all, but then I couldn't bring myself to put it on. I caved and gave into my need for black."

"Don't tell me you're going as a vampire?"

"Guilty. Not original, I know, but if I can't drink, I want to be comfortable."

I chuckled. "And Gavin?"

"His sense of humor seriously deteriorated once he started working for his mom in the morgue—or so he says. Gavin is going as a zombie, and I, for one, am looking forward to doing his makeup."

"I thought you'd go as a couple. As in, you'd match."

"Matching is tacky. I mean, it is except for someone your age."

"Seriously? I'm only eight years older than you."

"Just saying."

I understood her concern, but Jaxson was okay with it. "Let's finish putting these supplies away. Then I want to check with Aunt Fern to make sure there isn't something else she needs me to do."

AFTER DONNING MY costume the next evening, I kind of felt silly when I looked in the mirror. Supergirl? What had I been thinking? I wore a costume when I waitressed, but going as my Glinda the Good Witch persona wouldn't be in the Halloween spirit. Picking a super hero didn't fit my personality either, but Jaxson had suggested it. Why I listened to him, I don't know, though it could have been because I was always calling him my superman.

Iggy waddled into the bedroom and looked up at me. "Can I come to the party?"

Iggy was my pink, super sleuth iguana. He was my also familiar, and we'd been together about fifteen years. "There will be food, music, and alcohol. To be honest, I don't trust anyone to pay enough attention not to step on you."

"You know I can stay out of the way. And I have that camouflaged outfit that Aunt Fern made for me."

"That is a costume, for sure, but it will make you more susceptible to being hurt." So what if he could stick to the wall?

Before he could come up with another argument, a knock sounded on the door. "That's Jaxson." I rushed out of my bedroom, and when I pulled open the door, I sucked in a breath. "Wow. You look great."

He grinned, stepped inside, and kissed me. "Let me see your costume."

I spun around, a bit self-conscious. I was chunky and probably should have gone as a ghost and worn a white sheet to cover my curves. "It's a little tight."

"Are you kidding? You look great." He looked over at Iggy. "Why aren't you dressed, bud?"

"See?" my sassy iguana tossed back. "Jaxson wants me to come."

I knew when I was defeated. "Okay, but don't get in anyone's way."

He did his circle dance of joy. "I won't."

His costume was in my bedroom closet. Once I retrieved it, I put it on him. I had to admit, he looked cute. "Do you want some green face paint?"

"Yes, please. I'd like to look normal at least one day a year."

"No one will think you're special if you're green, you know." I loved the fact that he was pink.

"I'm good with that. Maybe no one will recognize me."

"Sure, they will. How many other iguanas have you seen in this town?"

"A lot. Okay, a few."

More like none. It didn't matter. I just wanted Iggy to be happy. "And Aimee? Won't she feel left out?"

Iggy stared at me. "I guess, but she can't get out of the way like I can."

Aimee was a cat that Aunt Fern had adopted. By mistake, this cat had been given the gift of speech. If I had to guess, Iggy used the idea she might be trampled on as an excuse not to invite her. My familiar loved to be the special one at a party.

Someone knocked on my aunt's door across the hall from my apartment. It probably was her new boyfriend, Peter Upton. I didn't know much about the man, but he made my aunt happy, and that was what was important.

I turned to Jaxson. "We have the first shift. Ready?"

"You bet."

I'd already checked that the decorations around the restaurant were all set to go. Aunt Fern had closed the Tiki Hut two house ago to allow some service to clear out the tables and chairs, and I couldn't wait for everyone to see what we'd accomplished.

As promised, my dad's crew had delivered the coffin. With the red light focused on the interior, I had to say the vampire looked so real it almost creeped me out.

Jaxson and Drake had set up the projector that shone the ghosts on the ceiling. Add in the pumpkins and the fans blowing dry ice over the cemetery, and the Tiki Hut Grill had been transformed into a scary but magical wonderland.

To further enhance the ambiance, Aunt Fern insisted we buy a few mannequins and dress them in locally themed Halloween costumes. Since Witch's Cove was situated on the

Gulf of Mexico, she'd dressed one in a shark outfit. Yes, she has a warped sense of humor. Dave Sanders, the owner of the Witch's Cove Dive Shop, donated his mannequin who was wearing a diving suit. To make the evening even more fun, Aunt Fern had hired a live band.

We'd set up two tables—one out front of the restaurant and one in back—to collect the party fee of twenty dollars. The money covered one trip to the buffet and two drinks. The Fire Marshall said we had to keep total attendance to one hundred people or less, which meant we needed to communicate with the table in back to make sure we didn't go over our limit.

Jaxson and I had signed up to take the first shift in front, because it was the most hectic time. Jaxson would handle the money and place a white band on the person's wrist, while I would hand out the food and drink tokens after checking the IDs, if necessary.

I nudged him. "Here comes the sheriff. Or at least I think that is Steve." He was wearing a Captain Hook costume, complete with a large hat, fake mustache, and an eyepatch. His date, who I believe was Misty Willows, the sheriff over in Liberty, dressed as Peter Pan. They looked really cute together.

"Glinda, Jaxson," the sheriff said. "Forty for the two of us, right?"

"That's right." Jaxson took the money, while I pressed my clicker twice and then handed them their tokens. "Enjoy the party."

I didn't have to check their IDs since I knew who they were. The next group had costumes that covered their faces.

One wore a Spiderman costume, another was Batman, and a third was Olaf from the movie *Frozen*. I checked their drivers' licenses and had to assume they belonged to the person holding the card. Considering their rather muscled bodies, they weren't high school kids. "Have fun."

"Thanks, little lady." That deep voice definitely belonged to an adult male.

Just as I was about to chat with Jaxson, a second wave of people arrived. First in line were Miriam and Maude Daniels, who were dressed as Raggedy Ann and Andy. They, too, looked adorable. Right behind them was Rihanna and Gavin. At five feet ten inches, my cousin made a rather imposing vampire.

"The white face makeup and heavy black eye makeup are perfect," I said. As was the black cape and red vest over the white shirt.

"Thanks. I had fun with it." She flashed me her fangs.

"Sweet."

I checked out Gavin. His outfit made him almost unrecognizable. Rihanna had done a great job making him look like he had real cuts and bruises on his face. I handed them their buffet and soft drink tokens and told them to enjoy the party.

For the next forty-five minutes, we had a non-stop flow of people. While I had thought Deputy Nash Solano would dress up as a werewolf, since he was one in real life, he chose to come as a vampire, too. While his costume matched Rihanna's, he didn't have nearly the same amount of black eyeliner that she did. "I like the teeth, but you might have a hard time enjoying our buffet with them in."

He winked. "Trust me, I'll take them out." Nash fished

out his money, and I gave him the tokens in exchange.

Once he stepped inside, two of our evening servers came outside. "You guys can go in and have some fun. We'll take over."

I handed her the clicker. "Just let the person at the back know when you reach fifty, so the two of you can make sure you don't go over one hundred."

"Will do."

We both stood. I couldn't wait for my first dance with Jaxson. Tonight was going to be epic.

The Pink Pumpkin Party (book 7 of A Witch's Cove Mystery) is available.

Buy on Amazon or read for FREE on Kindle Unlimited

THE END

A WITCH'S COVE MYSTERY (Paranormal Cozy Mystery)

PINK Is The New Black (book 1)

A PINK Potion Gone Wrong (book 2)

The Mystery of the PINK Aura (book 3)

Box Set (books 1-3)

Sleuthing In The PINK (book 4)

Not in The PINK (book 5)

Gone in the PINK of an Eye (book 6)

Box Set (books 4-6)

The Pink Pumpkin Party (book 7)

Mistletoe with a Pink Bow (book 8)

HIDDEN REALMS OF SILVER LAKE

(Paranormal Romance)

Awakened By Flames (book 1)

Seduced By Flames (book 2)

Kissed By Flames (book 3)

Destiny In Flames (book 4)

Box Set (books 1-4)

Passionate Flames (book 5)

Ignited By Flames (book 6)

Touched By Flames (book 7)

Box Set (books 5-7)

Bound By Flames (book 8)

Fueled By Flames (book 9)

Scorched By Flames (book 10)

FOUR SISTERS OF FATE: HIDDEN REALMS OF SILVER LAKE (Paranormal Romance)

Poppy (book 1)

Primrose (book 2)

Acacia (book 3)

Magnolia (book 4)

Box Set (books 1-4)

Jace (book 5)

Tanner (book 6)

WERES AND WITCHES OF SILVER LAKE

(Paranormal Romance)

A Magical Shift (book 1)

Catching Her Bear (book 2)

Surge of Magic (book 3)

The Bear's Forbidden Wolf (book 4)

Her Reluctant Bear (book 5)

Freeing His Tiger (book 6)

Protecting His Wolf (book 7)

Waking His Bear (book 8)

Melting Her Wolf's Heart (book 9)

Her Wolf's Guarded Heart (book 10)

His Rogue Bear (book 11)

Box Set (books 1-4)

Box Set (books 5-8)

Reawakening Their Bears (book 12)

PACK WARS (Paranormal Romance)

Training Their Mate (book 1)

Claiming Their Mate (book 2)

Rescuing Their Virgin Mate (book 3)

Box Set (books 1-3)

Loving Their Vixen Mate (book 4)

Fighting For Their Mate (book 5)

Enticing Their Mate (book 6)

Box Set (books 1-4)
Complete Box Set (books 1-6)

HIDDEN HILLS SHIFTERS
(Paranormal Romance)
An Unexpected Diversion (book 1)
Bare Instincts (book 2)
Shifting Destinies (book 3)
Embracing Fate (book 4)
Promises Unbroken (book 5)
Bare 'N Dirty (book 6)
Hidden Hills Shifters Complete Box Set (books 1-6)

MONTANA PROMISES
(Full length contemporary Romance)
Promises of Mercy (book 1)
Foundations For Three (book 2)
Montana Fire (book 3)
Montana Promises Box Set (books 1-3)
Hart To Hart (Book 4)
Burning Seduction (Book 5)
Montana Promises Complete Box Set (books 1-5)

ROCK HARD, MONTANA
(contemporary romance novellas)
Montana Desire (book 1)
Awakening Passions (book 2)

PLEDGED TO PROTECT
(contemporary romantic suspense)
From Panic To Passion (book 1)

From Danger To Desire (book 2)
From Terror To Temptation (book 3)
Pledged To Protect Box Set (books 1-3)

BURIED SERIES
(contemporary romantic suspense)
Buried Alive (book 1)
Buried Secrets (book 2)
Buried Deep (book 3)
The Buried Series Complete Box Set (books 1-3)

A NASH MYSTERY
(Contemporary Romance)
Sidearms and Silk(book 1)
Black Ops and Lingerie(book 2)
A Nash Mystery Box Set (books 1-2)

STARTER SETS (Romance)
Contemporary
Paranormal

Author Bio

Love it HOT and STEAMY? Sign up for my newsletter and receive MONTANA DESIRE for FREE. smarturl.it/o4cz93?IQid=MLite

OR Are you a fan of quirky PARANORMAL COZY MYSTERIES? Sign up for this newsletter. smarturl.it/CozyNL

Not only do I love to read, write, and dream, I'm an extrovert. I enjoy being around people and am always trying to understand what makes them tick. Not only must my romance books have a happily ever after, I need characters I can relate to. My men are wonderful, dynamic, smart, strong, and the best lovers in the world (of course).

My Paranormal Cozy Mysteries are where I let my imagination run wild with witches and a talking pink iguana who believes he's a real sleuth.

I believe I am the luckiest woman. I do what I love and I have a wonderful, supportive husband, who happens to be hot!

Fun facts about me

(1) I'm a math nerd who loves spreadsheets. Give me numbers and I'll find a pattern.

(2) I live on a Costa Rica beach!

(3) I also like to exercise. Yes, I know I'm odd.

I love hearing from readers either on FB or via email (hint, hint).

Social Media Sites

Website:
www.velladay.com

FB:
facebook.com/vella.day.90

Twitter:
@velladay4

Gmail:
velladayauthor@gmail.com

Made in the USA
Las Vegas, NV
29 July 2021